NO TU

Frank, Joe, and Mingma were driving along a narrow road with a sharp drop-off on the right. Sitting in the right front seat of Mingma's rickshaw, Joe could see that the muddy slope plunged almost straight down to a tree-filled ravine several hundred feet below.

"Wow," said Frank from the backseat. "There's barely room for two cars to pass on this road."

Joe was the first to spot the approaching car. It seemed to pick up speed as it came closer. "That guy better slow down," he muttered angrily.

Mingma steered the rickshaw closer to the edge to give the car room to pass them.

Joe sucked in his breath as the oncoming car suddenly careened toward them at full speed. There was no room to maneuver, and no time to stop.

"Watch out!" Mingma called.

Shooting past them, the car clipped their rear wheel. The rickshaw spun out of control and headed straight for the edge of the precipice.

Books in THE HARDY BOYS CASEFILES™ Series

#1	DEAD ON TARGET	#73	BAD RAP
#2	EVIL, INC.	#74	ROAD PIRATES
#3	CULT OF CRIME	#75	NO WAY OUT
#4	THE LAZARUS PLOT	#76	TAGGED FOR TERROR
#5	EDGE OF DESTRUCTION	#77	SURVIVAL RUN
#6	THE CROWNING TERROR	#78	THE PACIFIC CONSPIRACY
#7	DEATHGAME	#79	DANGER UNLIMITED
#8	SEE NO EVIL	#80	DEAD OF NIGHT
#9	THE GENIUS THIEVES	#81	SHEER TERROR
#12	PERFECT GETAWAY	#82	POISONED PARADISE
#13	THE BORGIA DAGGER	#83	TOXIC REVENGE
#14	TOO MANY TRAITORS	#84	FALSE ALARM
#29	THICK AS THIEVES	#85	WINNER TAKE ALL
#30	THE DEADLIEST DARE	#86	VIRTUAL VILLAINY
#32	BLOOD MONEY	#87	DEAD MAN IN DEADWOOD
#33	COLLISION COURSE	#88	INFERNO OF FEAR
#35	THE DEAD SEASON	#89	DARKNESS FALLS
#37	DANGER ZONE	#90	DEADLY ENGAGEMENT
#41	HIGHWAY ROBBERY	#91	HOT WHEELS
#42	THE LAST LAUGH	#92	SABOTAGE AT SEA
#44	CASTLE FEAR	#93	MISSION: MAYHEM
#45	IN SELF-DEFENSE	#94	A TASTE FOR TERROR
#46	FOUL PLAY	#95	ILLEGAL PROCEDURE
#47	FLIGHT INTO DANGER	#96	AGAINST ALL ODDS
#48	ROCK 'N' REVENGE	#97	PURE EVIL
#49	DIRTY DEEDS	#98	MURDER BY MAGIC
#50	POWER PLAY	#99	FRAME-UP
#52	UNCIVIL WAR	#100	TRUE THRILLER
#53	WEB OF HORROR	#101	PEAK OF DANGER
#54	DEEP TROUBLE	#102	WRONG SIDE OF THE LAW
#55	BEYOND THE LAW		
#56	HEIGHT OF DANGER	#103	CAMPAIGN OF CRIME
#57	TERROR ON TRACK	#104	WILD WHEELS
#60	DEADFALL	#105	LAW OF THE JUNGLE
#61	GRAVE DANGER	#106	SHOCK JOCK
#62	FINAL GAMBIT	#107	FAST BREAK
#63	COLD SWEAT	#108	BLOWN AWAY
#64	ENDANGERED SPECIES	#109	MOMENT OF TRUTH
#65	NO MERCY	#115	CAVE TRAP
#66	THE PHOENIX EQUATION	#116	ACTING UP
		#117	BLOOD SPORT
#69	MAYHEM IN MOTION	#118	THE LAST LEAP
#71	REAL HORROR		

Available from ARCHWAY Paperbacks

THE HARDY BOYS

CASEFILES™
NO. 112

CLIFF-HANGER

FRANKLIN W. DIXON

AN ARCHWAY PAPERBACK
Published by POCKET BOOKS
New York London Toronto Sydney Tokyo Singapore

AN ARCHWAY PAPERBACK *Original*

An Archway Paperback published by
POCKET BOOKS, a division of Simon & Schuster Inc.
1230 Avenue of the Americas, New York, NY 10020

Copyright © 1996 by Simon & Schuster Inc.
Produced by Mega-Books, Inc.

ISBN: 0-671-50453-3

First Archway Paperback printing June 1996

10 9 8 7 6 5 4 3 2

THE HARDY BOYS, AN ARCHWAY PAPERBACK and colophon are registered trademarks of Simon & Schuster Inc.

THE HARDY BOYS CASEFILES is a trademark of Simon & Schuster Inc.

Cover photograph from "The Hardy Boys" Series © 1995 Nelvana Limited/Marathon Productions S.A. All Rights Reserved.

Logo design ™ & © 1995 by Nelvana Limited. All Rights Reserved.
Printed in the U.S.A.

IL 6+

CLIFF-HANGER

Chapter

1

Joe Hardy felt his heart pounding as he fought for breath. He clung precariously to the rock face, his fingers clutching a hairline crack. He had climbed almost a hundred feet up the sheer granite, but now he was stuck. He couldn't see a safe way past the overhang that blocked his route to the top.

He glanced down to where his brother, Frank, stood far below at the base of the cliff, along with two companions. Joe's muscles tensed involuntarily. He hadn't thought about how far down it was. He dug his fingers even more tightly into the hairline crack, ignoring the pain.

Then he took a deep breath and forced himself to relax. "Just resting," he called down to the others. He was glad they were too far away to see him sweating.

Frank Hardy watched his brother's progress from below, wondering why he hadn't moved in five minutes.

They were rock climbing near Kathmandu, the capital of the kingdom of Nepal. They had come at the invitation of their Nepalese Sherpa friend, Mingma, who was standing next to Frank. Mingma, who was in his late teens, was much smaller than the six-foot-one Frank. While Frank was long and lean, Mingma was solid and stocky. He stood just over five feet, and his broad face was topped with a bushy head of black hair.

Several years earlier, Mingma had come to Bayport to stay with relatives for a year. The Hardys took him under their wing from his first day at school and taught him everything they knew about how to live like an American teenager. When Mingma's relatives had offered to return the favor, Frank and Joe had jumped at the chance.

Frank's other companion was Mingma's uncle Pasang, a former Sherpa mountaineering guide who had come along to show the Hardys the finer points of climbing. The Sherpas were a mountain people from the eastern part of Nepal who had become famous worldwide as guides and porters for climbers on expeditions into the Himalayas, even some up Mount Everest.

That day's climbing trip was practice for a longer expedition that the Hardys and their friends planned to make.

Pasang's sharp face showed the wear of a long, hard life in the mountains. Despite his stern manner, the Hardys had found him to be a patient instructor. At the moment, he had his keen eyes trained on Joe.

"Not that one!" Pasang called out as Joe reached up to grab a rock that jutted out above him. Frank sucked in his breath as he saw the rock come loose in Joe's hand. Caught off balance, Joe lost his grip with his other hand and began to slide down.

Joe clung to the rock face desperately with his hands and feet. After sliding several feet, he managed to hook his fingers into another crack and bring himself to a stop. Below, Frank breathed a sigh of relief and tightened his grip on the belay rope that would have supported his brother in the event of a fall.

As the belayer, Frank's job was to monitor this rope. From his hand, the rope ran all the way up the cliff to Joe, passing through a series of metal clips that were anchored to the rock every ten feet or so. Joe had carefully positioned these clips on the face on his way up. Climbers called this placing protection.

"Just making sure you guys were awake down

there," Joe called to the others, hoping they didn't hear his voice quaver.

He moved sideways, looking for another way up, and came to a narrow rock chimney where the walls closed in on three sides. By bracing his hands and feet on opposite sides of the chimney, he was able to inch slowly upward. Soon he stood on top of the cliff.

"Piece of cake," he called down. "Off belay," he added, remembering the terminology Pasang had taught him to indicate that he no longer needed the protection of the belay rope.

Frank and Joe now swapped roles. Frank followed Joe up the same route, while Joe belayed from above. As Frank climbed, he removed each of the anchors Joe had placed. These included various chocks and other spring-loaded devices that were wedged into cracks to secure the rope. This way, the Hardys left the cliff as they had found it.

Both Hardys now stood on top of the cliff. "Now comes the good part." Joe grinned.

Joe wrapped the climbing rope around a tree that stood near the top of the cliff. He called out, "Rope," to warn the others below. Then he threw both ends of the rope down to the ground and clipped it to a harness around his waist.

With the rope gripped firmly in his hands, Joe backed himself toward the edge of the cliff. "See you at the bottom," he said. Then he was gone.

Frank winced as he watched Joe half fall, half slide down the rope, his feet bouncing off the cliff every ten to fifteen feet. Frank followed at a more controlled speed.

The climb over, all four piled into Mingma's rickshaw for the drive back to Kathmandu. The vehicle resembled a large three-wheeled motor scooter with a roof. Sitting in the back, the Hardys had a chance to admire the scenery as the road wound through lush green hills and tiny villages.

When they arrived in the city, they dropped Pasang off and headed for Mingma's home. Mingma's father, Lapka, met them at the door.

"Namaste," he said, using the traditional Nepalese greeting. "Dinner is prepared."

They sat at the table, and Mingma's mother, Ama Sundeki, brought out steaming plates of food. The main course was *dhal bhat tarkaari,* rice with lentil beans and vegetable curry, along with a special delicacy: *raagaku maasu,* or water buffalo. After a long day of hiking and climbing, they ate heartily.

"This evening there is a lecture at the Annapurna Hotel," Mingma told the Hardys during dinner. "The American climber Roland Swain is going to speak."

"I read about him in a climbing magazine," Frank said excitedly. "Isn't he leading an expedition to climb a major peak?"

"Yes," Mingma answered. "The mountain is one of the highest in the world. It is called Yeti's Tower, named after the abominable snowman, the yeti. Many people claim to have spotted this creature in the area."

"The abominable snowman?" Joe's ears pricked up. "Do people really believe in that?"

Mingma's father turned to Joe. "Many people take the legend of the yeti seriously," he said.

"Anyway, nobody has ever made it to the top of Yeti's Tower," Mingma continued. "The mountain itself has a legendary status among mountaineers. Bad luck comes to every party that tries to climb it."

"Swain headed an expedition that tried. It ended in disaster," Frank said. "The whole group was wiped out by an avalanche."

"That's right." Mingma nodded. "Only Swain and two others survived. That was six years ago, and nobody has even attempted the mountain since. The government refused to give anyone permission, until this year."

"So Swain is returning to conquer the mountain that defeated him before," Joe observed. "Pretty dramatic stuff."

"One man's drama is another man's folly," Mingma's father muttered. "He should have learned his lesson the first time."

Hearing this, Frank and Joe exchanged glances. They had both noted the similarities and contrasts between Pasang and Mingma's father, Lapka. The two brothers shared a strong resemblance, but Lapka's face was softened by a life spent indoors. He walked with a slight limp and seemed to disapprove of anything connected to mountain climbing.

As soon as dinner was over, the Hardys and Mingma piled into the rickshaw and headed for the Annapurna Hotel, which was downtown, just off Kathmandu's famous Durbar Square. By the time they arrived, many of the merchants had gone home for the day, but the square was still humming with activity. Wandering among the tourists and hawkers, the Hardys noticed several men in colorful attire. These, Mingma explained, were *saddhus,* or holy men.

Crossing the square on the way to the hotel, Frank and Joe were struck by the towering Maju Deval temple across from the Old Royal Palace. The triple-roofed temple was perched on a high base.

Stairs on all four sides allowed visitors to approach from any direction. Each of the three roofs was supported by ornately carved wooden struts.

A crowd had already gathered as Frank, Joe, and Mingma entered the hotel lecture hall. After a brief introduction from the president of a local mountaineering society, a burly man with sandy hair and a broad, high forehead approached the podium. He got right to the point.

"The Nepal Himalayas present the ultimate challenge to the world's mountaineers," Roland Swain began, his voice resonating through the room. "Eight of the ten highest mountains in the world are right here in Nepal. Even as we speak, our attempt to conquer one of the last of those great peaks is already under way."

Swain went on to describe his last tragic journey to Yeti's Tower, six years before. When the climbers were still several thousand feet from the summit, an avalanche had thundered down the mountain, killing nine members of the party. The victims included the expedition's leaders, Ernst and Luther Waldmann.

A man in the audience raised his hand. "Sir, do you have hopes of finding any remains of the Waldmann expedition? It is widely known that no bodies were ever recovered."

Swain gave the man a flat look. "The goal of our expedition is to climb the mountain."

Another man stood up on the far side of the room. "What about the secret expedition you made to the mountain last year? What was your goal then?"

Recognizing the speaker, Joe elbowed his brother in the ribs. It was Mingma's uncle Pasang.

Swain glared down at Pasang. "I don't know

what you're talking about," he said coldly. "I haven't made any secret expeditions. And you of all people have no business being here."

"It all worked out very well for you," Pasang shot back. "I became your scapegoat, and you became a rich man."

Before he could continue, three men in matching jackets quickly surrounded Pasang. The smallest of the three spoke to Pasang in low, rapid-fire Nepali while pointing toward the door. Frank guessed they must be employees of the hotel. Pasang faced them defiantly for a moment, then departed without another word.

Mingma was stunned. "I must go after my uncle," he said to the Hardys. "Please wait." The Hardys nodded as he left.

As Swain continued his lecture, Frank saw two more men go out the same door Mingma and Pasang had used. One was tall, with light hair, the other much shorter. Otherwise, he didn't get a good look at them. Frank suppressed an urge to follow them.

Twenty-five minutes later the lecture was over, and Mingma still had not returned. When he finally did reappear, he acted troubled. "My uncle told me that he would be going away," he said simply, then grew silent.

"That's all?" Frank pressed. "He didn't say anything else?"

Mingma hesitated before answering. "He told

me that when the time was right, I would know where to find him. Then he gave me his gold watch and asked me to keep it for him. This watch is very precious to him. Normally, he keeps it with him at all times."

Mingma paused. "He always said that he wanted me to have the watch—but only after he died."

The Hardys were burning with curiosity as they headed home. What had prompted Pasang's comments? What did he mean about being made a scapegoat? Not wanting to pry, they waited for Mingma to volunteer an explanation. But Mingma said nothing, and they went to sleep with their questions unanswered.

The next morning at breakfast, the Hardys were still thinking about Pasang's words when they heard a loud knock on the door. Mingma's father got up to answer. After a moment, they heard him speaking in the front room.

His voice sounded shrill as he greeted the visitors.

A sharp, nasal voice answered, Mingma translated. "It's a National Police lieutenant named Tamang," he whispered. "They are looking for my uncle Pasang. He is wanted for questioning."

The Hardys and Mingma were on their feet in a second. Charging into the front room, they were stopped in their tracks by several police officers armed with submachine guns.

On the far side of the room, Mingma's father stood facing the lieutenant, who wore a towering hat that made him look taller than the others. His chest was decorated with badges. After dismissing the Hardys with a glance, Tamang turned back to Mingma's father.

"According to Pasang's family, he hasn't been home since yesterday. Is he here?"

"Why do you want to question him?" Mingma's father demanded.

For a long moment Lieutenant Tamang said nothing. Instead he looked around the room, as if he thought that one of them might turn out to be Pasang in disguise. "Pasang is wanted for attempted murder," he said finally. "He tried to kill the American mountain climber Roland Swain."

Chapter

2

FRANK AND JOE COULDN'T BELIEVE their ears. Pasang was wanted for murder? Frank's mind was spinning as he caught Joe's eye. He knew they were both thinking the same thing: Pasang may have been upset the night before, but the gentle, firm Sherpa would never have tried to kill anybody.

Mingma was defiant. "My uncle is not a murderer," he said fiercely.

"Last night someone attacked Roland Swain in his room at the Annapurna Hotel," Lieutenant Tamang continued, ignoring Mingma. "Mr. Swain woke just as the attacker was about to bury a mountaineering ax in his skull. Luckily, he was able to defend himself. He seized the ax, and the attacker fled."

12

"What evidence do you have against Pasang?" Frank asked.

Lieutenant Tamang threw Frank a startled glance. "Pasang was seen by the hotel staff," he answered. "He made several attempts to get inside Mr. Swain's room."

"You mean he tried to break in?" Joe asked.

"He badgered the hotel employees to wake Mr. Swain. When they refused, he tried to sneak past them and had to be escorted off the premises."

"That hardly sounds like grounds for a murder accusation," Frank said. "Did anyone witness the attack? Were there fingerprints on the ax?"

"That is Nepalese police business," the lieutenant snapped, irritated by the Hardys' questions. "We are not here to defend our case. We are looking for Pasang. Is he here?"

Mingma's father shook his head. "We have not seen him," he said. "But wherever he is, I know he will come forward to prove his innocence."

Tamang turned to his men. "Search the house," he commanded.

Mingma's mother had been standing in the back of the room. She now came forward to face the lieutenant. "Pasang is not here," she said, her tone soft but firm.

Lieutenant Tamang relented. "Very well. If you see him, you must contact the police immediately. Wherever he went, we will find him," he added. With a last glance at the Hardys, he turned to leave.

The Hardys and Mingma watched from the doorway as the police departed. Crossing under a large tree, the lieutenant looked up and muttered an oath. The Hardys saw that his anger was directed at a large monkey crouched in the branches above.

Joe couldn't help but chuckle. "Looks like the monkey's giving him a hard time." The monkey shrieked at the lieutenant, baring its teeth.

"We often see this monkey in our yard," Mingma explained. "We call him Gurkha." The Hardys had already noticed that semiwild monkeys were common in the streets and temples of Kathmandu.

Mingma's father was still shaking his head as they closed the door. "This cannot be," he said. "It just cannot be." He went upstairs to his room and closed the door behind him. Mingma's mother followed, apologizing to the Hardys.

Mingma spoke to the Hardys in low tones. "You must excuse my father," he said. "Nepal is not like the United States. In your country, there are violent crimes in the news every day. Here, such things are a great shock."

"Attempted murder is shocking anywhere," Frank replied.

"My uncle would never hurt anyone...." Mingma's voice trailed off. The Hardys nodded agreement, but they could see that their friend was thinking of his uncle's last words the day before.

"Last night," Joe asked, "did your uncle say where he was going, or why?"

"All he said was that when the time was right, I would understand. Nothing more."

"Don't take this the wrong way," Frank said, "but obviously something was up yesterday between Swain and your uncle. If we knew what was going on, maybe we could help."

Mingma glanced upstairs toward his father's room and took a deep breath. "My father thinks we shouldn't talk about family business," Mingma said. "You see, my uncle was with Swain during his last attempt to climb Yeti's Tower, six years ago. He was one of the three who survived the avalanche, along with Swain and another Sherpa named Gyaltsen."

Joe let out a low whistle. "Pasang was one of the survivors of the Waldmann expedition?"

Mingma nodded. "The avalanche occurred when a rope came loose. A climber fell onto an unstable cornice and set the avalanche in motion. My uncle was the one who had set the rope, so he was blamed. No formal accusation was ever made, but his reputation was ruined, and he had to retire from professional mountaineering."

"So that's what your uncle meant about being

a scapegoat," Frank said. "Is it true they never found any of the bodies?"

Mingma shook his head. "At the time bad weather made any search impossible, and afterward the authorities never bothered. The mountain is very remote, very dangerous. Most people in Nepal don't believe it's worth risking lives to recover bodies."

"Do you know what your uncle meant about Swain making secret trips to Yeti's Tower and becoming a rich man?" Joe asked.

Mingma shook his head.

"If your uncle really did go away, it doesn't look good for him. He's disappeared just when the police started looking for him," Frank said.

Mingma pulled a gold object out of his pocket and clutched it tightly in his hand. It was his uncle's watch. "That's why I didn't tell the police about my conversation with my uncle last night."

"If your uncle is in some kind of trouble, the police might be able to help," Frank suggested.

"They'll most likely throw him in jail," Mingma said. "You saw how the police were this morning. There's been a crime, so they need to arrest somebody. They don't care if they arrest the wrong person." He gazed again at the watch in his hand. "That's strange," he said. "The watch doesn't seem to be working."

"I've done a little tinkering with watches before," Joe said. "If you want, I can try to fix it."

"Perhaps," Mingma said, turning the watch over in his hand. "I have to apologize to you," he continued. "I'm afraid we'll have to cancel our plans to go mountaineering."

"Forget our plans," Joe said. "We have to figure out where your uncle went."

"And who attacked Swain," Frank added.

"I can't ask you to become involved," Mingma objected. "My father would never permit it."

"We're already involved," Joe said.

Mingma thought for a moment. "Well, I had planned for us to go to the Ministry of Tourism today to pick up your trekking permits. Now we have another reason to go. I have a friend there who may be able to help us."

The Hardys knew that the government of Nepal required all foreigners who ventured into the mountains to carry trekking permits. But as they climbed into the rickshaw, they wondered what other purpose Mingma had for going to the ministry.

On the drive there, Joe was struck by the rich contrasts of Kathmandu. The city was a living museum. The rickshaw wound past carved temples that were hundreds of years old, along crowded streets now choked with twentieth-century cars, buses, and exhaust fumes.

Entering the ministry, Mingma led them into a small office where a young man stood up to greet them. "Frank, Joe, this is Pertemba."

17

Pertemba shook hands with the Hardys. "Welcome to Nepal," he said. "I have your trekking permits ready." He handed each of them an envelope.

Mingma looked around as if to make sure nobody was listening. "I need to ask you a favor," he said in a low voice. "I would like to see the official records of the Waldmann expedition."

There followed an urgent exchange in Nepalese. The Hardys heard Mingma use the names Swain and Pasang, and they sensed that Pertemba was uncomfortable with Mingma's request.

Finally, Pertemba agreed. "I will do my best, but I'll need a few days," he said, speaking in English again. "Come back Tuesday or Wednesday."

After thanking Pertemba, they left the ministry and walked past the central telegraph office toward the post office.

"Access to the peaks is strictly controlled by the government," Mingma explained. "Until the 1950s no foreigners were allowed into the mountains at all. Even today the world's top climbers wait years for permission to climb the major peaks. The competition is intense."

Joe was impressed. "You could say it's the World Series of mountaineering."

"You could." Mingma nodded. "Anyhow, Pertemba said that Yeti's Tower is especially sensitive, because it is in a remote part of Nepal, close to the border with Tibet."

They went to the post office, where Frank and Joe mailed several postcards.

"Chet will eat his heart out when he hears that Kathmandu is the best place in all of Asia to get homemade apple pie," Joe said with a grin. Chet Morton was one of the Hardys' best friends back in Bayport, and he was known for his large appetite.

"Callie, too," Frank said, referring to his girlfriend, Callie Shaw. "I don't know how hot she'd be to climb mountains, but she'd love Kathmandu."

Leaving the post office, Frank headed toward a row of street vendors. Joe followed, wrinkling his nose. A person could buy anything from live chickens to fake Rolex watches. Frank walked up to one stall. Among a row of intricately decorated statues was an old brass watch, similar to the one Pasang had given Mingma.

"How much?" Frank asked.

The vendor gave Frank a predatory smile. "Today is your lucky day. I give you good price." He named a figure.

Frank shook his head. "Too rich for my blood." He started to walk away.

"Okay, wait," called the vendor. "I make a special price only for you."

Five minutes later the watch hung on a chain around Frank's neck.

"That was quite a discount you got," Joe commented as they headed back to where Mingma's rickshaw was parked.

"In Kathmandu, everything is negotiable," Mingma said.

Frank fingered his new watch during the ride home, thinking about Mingma's uncle Pasang. The Sherpa had survived a tragic climbing accident six years earlier only to take the blame for it. Now he was wanted for murder. Frank knew they had to help the man clear his name.

The door of Mingma's house was locked when they arrived. "Looks like nobody's home," Mingma said, unlocking it with his key. He pushed the door open and waved the Hardys in.

"I'm going upstairs to put my trekking permit in my bag," Joe told Frank as they entered. "I can take yours, too." Frank handed his permit to Joe, who headed upstairs for Mingma's room.

The walk-in closet where the Hardys had left their things was open. It was spacious inside but dark. Joe groped for a light switch but couldn't find it. Never mind, he thought. He'd be there for only a minute, and his eyes would adjust.

He knelt down and groped for his bag. His hand closed on what felt like a sock. Groping around some more, he realized that clothes were scattered all over the floor.

It was then that he heard a low hiss, like an intake of breath, coming from behind him.

He started to whirl around just as something

20

landed on him. He felt hot breath on the back of his neck and a pair of powerful arms wrap around his head and neck.

Caught off balance, he reeled backward and fell. A big hand was clamped over his mouth as he struggled to shake off his attacker.

Chapter

3

IN THE SEMIDARKNESS, Joe couldn't get a good look at his opponent. But he felt his long and hairy arms. Then he finally caught a glimpse of a big, grimacing mouth.

Joe relaxed for an instant to muster his strength. Then, in a single move, he grabbed the hairy arms, hurled them off, and leaped to his feet. His opponent had had enough and ran shrieking out the door, almost colliding with Frank and Mingma, who had rushed upstairs to see what was happening.

Joe's attacker was Gurkha, the monkey from the yard. The three of them watched as the monkey dashed out of Mingma's room, down the hallway, and out an open window at the far end.

"Nice work, Joe," Frank said, barely concealing a grin. "You really scared that monkey. What'd you do? Sneak up and whisper sweet nothings in his ear?"

Joe glared at his brother. "How was I supposed to know it was a monkey?" Then he grinned. "Actually, he kind of looks like that guy I wrestled at the state championships last year."

Mingma became serious. "I wonder how the window was opened," he said. "My parents would never leave it that way."

Frank took a close look. "Somebody forced it open," he said, pointing to where the lock had been damaged.

"You mean somebody broke in?" Mingma asked, suddenly concerned. "My parents—what if they were here?" he said, hurrying to check their room.

The Hardys fanned out to do a quick search. They quickly confirmed that the rest of the house was undisturbed.

"I'm sure your parents are fine," Joe told Mingma. "If something had happened to them, there would be signs of a struggle."

Returning to his room, Mingma went into his closet and flipped on the light. His dresser drawers hung open, and clothes were scattered all over the floor.

"They searched only Mingma's closet," Frank noted. "That's strange."

"Maybe we interrupted them before they could search the rest of the house," Joe suggested. "Anything seem to be missing?"

Mingma shook his head. "Nothing," he said as he began picking up his clothes. "For now, I'd rather my parents didn't know about this. They would be terribly upset, and my father would insist on calling the police, who would immediately suspect my uncle."

"Could it have been your uncle?" Joe asked.

"My uncle is welcome here anytime," Mingma said. "Why would he break in?"

The Hardys exchanged glances. "All right," Frank agreed. "We won't say anything to your parents, for now. But if anything else happens, we're going to have to tell them."

Mingma's parents arrived minutes later. They had gone out to buy groceries. His mother prepared dinner within an hour. There was little conversation at the table, and afterward everyone quickly retired. Lieutenant Tamang's visit that morning clearly had shaken up everybody.

"Tomorrow I'd like to visit my uncle's family," Mingma told the Hardys before they went to bed. "They live in the town of Patan, just across the river from Kathmandu."

When they woke the next morning, it was cool and rainy. They piled into the rickshaw without breakfast and set out for Patan. As they drove out of the city, Joe thought that the rain and fog made the narrow, ancient streets appear even more mysterious.

Twenty-five minutes later Mingma pulled up in front of a run-down building. The Hardys followed him up a single flight of stairs to a low wooden door at the end of a narrow hallway.

Pasang's wife, Tende Samnug, greeted them warmly. She wore a heavy wool shirt and a long, colorful apron. The Hardys gratefully accepted the warm mugs of *chiyaa*, or tea, that she offered. She was trying to put on a brave face, but the Hardys could see that the recent events had worn her down.

Mingma spoke with Tende Samnug for several minutes. Since she spoke little English, Mingma summarized her words for the Hardys. "She says that two days ago, just after Pasang returned from climbing with us, he received a visit from a Sherpa named Gyaltsen."

Joe recognized the name. "Didn't you say that Gyaltsen was the third survivor of the Waldmann expedition, along with Swain and your uncle?"

Mingma nodded. "That's right. After Gyaltsen's visit, my uncle became very upset. He left in a hurry and never came back."

"He must have gone to Swain's lecture, where we saw him," Frank said.

"I'm afraid so," Mingma said, hanging his

25

head. "Before he left, he told my aunt that he had a score to settle."

"Any idea what this Gyaltsen might have told your uncle to make him so upset?" Joe asked.

Mingma shrugged. "I met Gyaltsen once, but that was a couple of years ago. I didn't know they were still in touch."

A young girl came into the room. Joe guessed she was in her early teens. "Welcome," she said, speaking excellent English. "I am Namu, Pasang's eldest daughter." She smiled briefly at the Hardys, then handed Mingma a clipping from a newspaper written in English.

"My father saved this article. I know he thought it was important," she told him. Mingma read the clipping, then handed it to Frank.

The article described how the climber Roland Swain had recently inherited a fortune from the Austrian millionaire Arnold Waldmann. According to the article, Swain had come into the inheritance through his now-deceased mother, who had married Waldmann some years before, after the death of Swain's father.

"Listen to this," Frank read aloud. " 'The fortune would have gone to Waldmann's twin sons, Ernst and Luther, had they not died in an avalanche several years ago.' "

"That explains what Pasang meant about Swain becoming a rich man," Joe said. "Pasang must have thought Swain murdered his step-brothers and made it look like an accident."

Frank examined the article. "This clipping is several months old—which doesn't explain why Pasang waited until now to disappear."

Mingma and the Hardys stayed to finish their tea. They reassured Pasang's wife and daughter that they would find him and that there would be a good reason for his disappearance. Then they thanked their hosts for their hospitality and said goodbye. As they left, Joe caught a glimpse of Namu. She stood bravely next to her mother, but Joe could tell she was scared. She was probably wondering whether she would ever see her father again.

Outside, Mingma pointed to a nearby teahouse that his uncle went to daily. He suggested they go in and question the proprietor.

"Welcome, welcome," the man greeted Mingma. "It is good that you are here. A stranger has been asking for your uncle."

He led them to a table where a Nepalese man sat. The man had a narrow face with small eyes that darted around the room as they approached.

The proprietor addressed the stranger. "This is Mingma, Pasang's nephew. Perhaps he can help you."

The stranger jumped up, shifting uncomfortably. "*Namaste*, er, hello," he said. "I must be

27

going." He gathered his things and scurried out the door.

Frank stared after the stranger. In a country where nobody was ever in a hurry, the man seemed out of place. "That guy was jumpy," he said.

Joe nodded agreement. He turned to Mingma. "Any idea who he was?"

Mingma shook his head. "No."

Frank picked up a paper from the table. "Too bad," he said. "Mister Jumpy forgot his brochure." It was an advertisement for the Yeti Adventure Travel Company. "Explore the mysteries of the Legendary Yeti," it read.

They decided to stay and have lunch in the teahouse. After ordering, Mingma turned to the Hardys. "I think we should spend the rest of the day in Patan and stay with my uncle's family tonight. That way we can watch over them, and if anyone else comes asking for my uncle, we'll know. I have a feeling he might even try to come home for a visit himself."

Frank and Joe agreed. Mingma phoned home from the teahouse to tell his father what he planned.

They spent the afternoon wandering the streets around Pasang's home, looking for the nervous stranger they had nicknamed Jumpy or for any other unusual activity. Except for two uniformed men who drove by every few minutes in an unmarked car, the village was quiet. The police, it seemed, were also keeping an eye on Pasang's house.

After dinner in the teahouse, they returned to Pasang's apartment. Namu brought them blankets, and they stretched out on the living-room floor.

Mingma was still restless. "I think I'll wait up awhile, just to keep an eye on things. I'm not sleepy, anyhow."

"I don't mind taking a shift at watching. It'll give you a chance to sleep," Frank volunteered. "Wake me up in a few hours. You can use this to mark the time." He handed Mingma the watch he had bought, along with a small flashlight.

It seemed to Frank that he had barely closed his eyes when he felt Mingma shaking him. His tone was urgent. "Someone tried to break in!"

Frank sat bolt upright. Beside him, Joe rubbed his eyes and yawned. Mingma was shining the flashlight on one of the windows. It hung open.

"Whoever it was ran when I shone the light on him," he said.

The window opened onto a narrow alley backed by a high stone wall. There was no sign of any intruder by the time they made it outside.

"Let's split up," Joe suggested. "I'll go this way. You, go that way."

"Let's meet back here in ten minutes," Frank said as he and Mingma set off together.

"I'll take this branch," Mingma said when the alley split. Frank hesitated, then headed down the other branch.

He had gone roughly a hundred feet when he

heard a call for help coming from behind him. Moving at full speed, he retraced his steps and headed the way Mingma had gone.

Within a short distance, his way was blocked by a high wall. After taking a running start, he leaped up, hooked his fingers over the top of the wall, and pulled himself up.

In the moonlight he could make out a small courtyard below him. A figure lay still on the ground. Frank jumped down and bent over the figure. It was Mingma, and he was unconscious.

Then Frank heard a low growl.

Two large dogs appeared out of the blackness. They were darker than the shadows, barely discernible except for their fangs, which gleamed in the moonlight. Heads low to the ground, they split up and advanced like wolves circling in for the kill.

Frank knew he could make it back over the wall to safety, but he couldn't abandon Mingma.

He backed off several steps and succeeded in drawing the dogs away from Mingma. But now he was cornered. The dogs moved in, snarling.

He took another step backward and found himself up against the wall.

As Frank realized there was no way to save both himself and Mingma, the animals lunged for him.

Chapter

4

FRANK GROPED ALONG THE WALL for anything he could use to defend himself. One dog was almost on top of him, the other a step behind.

Just as the first dog leaped for his throat, Frank closed his right hand on what felt like a wooden handle. The beast was already in the air as Frank swung with all his might, not even knowing what he was swinging. As it moved in front of his eyes, Frank saw that it was a broom.

The dog let out a yelp as the broom whacked the side of its head, knocking the animal to one side.

Frank moved quickly, holding the broom in front of the second dog with both hands. Its powerful jaws locked on the wooden handle, nearly biting through it.

31

Frank twisted the handle, throwing the dog off balance, and sprang forward, escaping from the corner. Holding the broom in front of him, he moved around the yard, trying to stay in the open.

Again the dogs closed in, growling louder than before.

Abruptly, a light went on up above, and a female voice barked out a command. The dogs drew back but kept their eyes fixed squarely on Frank, who was panting now. Out of the corner of his eye, he saw a woman standing on a balcony.

Then a door opened at ground level, and a male voice called out in Nepali. Frank struggled to remember any phrases of the local language. *"Ma ali ali nepaali bolchhu,"* he said. "I only speak a little Nepali." He held his hands up to show that he meant no harm. "My friend is hurt," he added in English, gesturing with his head to where Mingma lay.

"Who are you?" the male voice asked, speaking in English now.

"My name is Frank Hardy. I'm an American. My friend is hurt," he repeated.

The female voice called from the balcony above, speaking in Nepali. Frank was unable to understand the conversation that followed.

"I am coming to check your friend," the male voice finally said. "Please do not make any move, or my wife will telephone the police."

The dogs still held Frank at bay as a man came out of the doorway and bent over Mingma, who gave out a low moan. A woman came out of the house carrying blankets, which they draped over Mingma.

Only then did the man approach Frank. "I am Mr. Chettri. Tell me how you came here and what happened to your friend—if he is your friend."

Frank recounted how he and Mingma had been chasing an intruder. "If you telephone my friend's family, they can confirm who we are," Frank finished, and gave them the number.

By this time Mingma was sitting up, rubbing his head. Another conversation in Nepali followed.

"Your friend's story seems to agree with yours," Mr. Chettri told Frank, shooing the dogs back inside the house. "I will go call his father."

While Mr. Chettri went back inside, Frank helped Mingma to his feet. Mingma explained that when the dogs had attacked, he'd tried to scramble back over the wall. "When I got to the top, my foot slipped," he said, "and I fell. That's all I remember. The fall must have knocked me out."

They went inside, and Mr. Chettri told Mingma that his father was on the way.

"My brother is still out in the alley somewhere," Frank told Mr. Chettri. "If you'll excuse me, I need to find him."

"I'd better go with you," Mr. Chettri offered. "We'll take the dogs. The alleys can be dangerous at night." Frank nodded and followed Mr. Chettri through a side gate that led into the alley.

They ran into Joe almost immediately. "You guys had me worried," Joe said. "When you didn't turn up, I was afraid I'd have to come and stage a dramatic rescue."

It took a long time for Mingma's father to arrive. "Getting a taxi at this hour to cross the river is not easy," he said to the Chettris, apologizing for the delay and thanking them repeatedly.

They were just about to leave when Mingma turned to Frank. "The watch that you loaned me last night—I just realized that it's gone. It must have fallen off my neck."

"It's probably back in the yard," Frank said, going to look. While waiting for him to return, Joe saw Mingma reach into his pocket. Mingma's relieved expression told Joe that he still had his uncle's gold watch.

"No sign of my watch," Frank said when he returned.

"It was so cheap," Joe said. "You can buy another one."

After stopping to tell Pasang's family about the break-in and their attempt to find the intruder, they headed back to Kathmandu in the rickshaw.

Mingma's father did not hide his displeasure during the drive.

"If there really was a trespasser," he said skeptically, "you should have telephoned the police. Sneaking around the city in the middle of the night can only lead to trouble."

The next morning the three sat in Mingma's room. The Hardys' friend was glum.

"When my father was my age, he went as a porter on an expedition to Mount Everest," Mingma said. "He slipped in a treacherous ice field and was injured. He was lucky not to be killed, but he did come away with a permanent limp." Mingma shook his head in frustration. "For this reason, he has always discouraged me from becoming a mountaineer or from taking any risks at all."

"Our aunt Gertrude is the same way," said Joe. "Always worrying."

Frank turned to Mingma. "It probably is a good idea for you to take your father's advice and rest, at least for this morning," he said. "And I have an idea how Joe and I can fill the time." He produced the brochure that the nervous stranger had left in the teahouse the day before. "I'd like to check out the Yeti Adventure Travel Company."

Mingma read the address on the brochure

"That's not far from here," he said, giving them directions.

The entrance to the office was off a narrow alleyway. A Nepalese man rose to greet them as they entered.

"Welcome," he said with an enthusiastic smile. "You would like to go on a tour? Perhaps a river safari to Chitwan National Park to see the very rare Indian rhinoceros?"

Joe placed the brochure on the counter. "We'd like to explore the mysteries of the yeti." He added, "As it says in your ad."

"Ah, yes, the yeti," the man said. "We have many packages available. How much time do you want to spend?"

As Joe spoke with the man, Frank checked out the office. One wall was decorated with photographs showing happy groups of tourists in different parts of Nepal.

Many of the photos features a big, square-jawed man with blond hair. Usually, he was posing with tourists. A few of the pictures seemed far older than the others and looked as if they had been taken in Africa. In them, the same man posed next to various big-game trophies. One picture showed him next to a dead lion.

"Who is this man?" Frank asked, pointing at one of the pictures.

"That is Mr. Richard Skelton, the proprietor. He is away on a scientific expedition."

"From the photos, he looks more like a hunter than a scientist," Frank commented.

"Where do your tours go?" Joe asked. "Is there one prime spot for yeti-watching?"

"We do not go 'yeti-watching,' " the man replied with a touch of scorn. "Our customers have an opportunity to build the scientific case for the existence of the yeti. We search for footprints and other tangible evidence and follow up accounts of possible sightings."

"What about that mountain called Yeti's Tower?" Frank asked. "That sounds like a good place to look for a yeti. Do any of your tours go there?"

"That would be difficult," the man said. "That is in a very remote area. Access is restricted by the government."

"None of your groups has ever gone there?" Frank said.

"Not recently." The salesman gave them a dry smile. "Do you want to book a tour now?"

"Not today," Joe said, "but we're definitely interested in finding out more about your tours."

"One last question," Frank said. "We'd like to find the man who gave us this brochure." Frank went on to describe "Jumpy" as best he could.

"Many people pass out our brochures, even though we don't pay them to. They hope that if

37

they bring in enough business, we'll give them a commission or even a job."

"Sounds like a tough life," Joe said.

"Yes. Unfortunately, we cannot afford to hire everybody," the man said. "Good afternoon."

"Give Mr. Skelton our best," Joe said as they left. "If we meet the yeti, we'll tell him to stop by."

Mingma was still in his room when they returned. "I need to get out of the house," he said. "There's a place called Nagarkot that I'd like to show you. Perhaps my uncle is there. Be sure to bring your binoculars, though, so we can do some sightseeing."

Once again they set out in Mingma's rickshaw. Nagarkot, Mingma explained, was a village on the rim of the Kathmandu Valley.

"My uncle has never really been happy living in a city," Mingma explained. "He was born in a remote village, near the base of Mount Everest. He often visits Nagarkot, because on a clear day he can see all the way to his home."

Joe was excited. "You mean we'll actually see Mount Everest, the highest mountain in the world?"

"Not only that," said Mingma, "you'll see eight of the ten highest mountains in the world."

The road climbed past terraced farms carved into steep hillsides. Not an inch of land was unused. The Hardys sensed the change as the thick smells of Kathmandu, far below them, gave way to crisp mountain air.

After weaving through a last stand of pine trees, they reached the village of Nagarkot, which was little more than a few buildings. Mingma parked the rickshaw and led them down a short path to a rocky point.

Frank and Joe were awed by the panorama spread out before them. The Himalayan range glistened white in the distance, stretching as far as they could see in either direction.

"Mount Everest is over there," Mingma said, pointing off to the right. "Altogether, the section of the range you're looking at is almost two hundred miles long."

"Exactly how high is Everest?" Joe asked.

"Just over twenty-nine thousand feet," Mingma said.

Frank gave a low whistle. "Twice as high as any mountain in the Rockies."

Joe pulled out his binoculars to scan the ridge. It was like looking at the moon. Even at that distance, he was able to make out sheer rock faces and jagged ridges covered with snow and ice. People had no business on it, he thought to himself.

His mind flashed on Pasang, who had climbed many of these mountains. He pictured him as a tiny speck of dust on one of those peaks. In a rare moment, Joe Hardy was at a loss for words.

After visiting Nagarkot for several hours, they started back to Kathmandu along a narrow road with a sharp dropoff on the right. Sitting in the right front seat of the rickshaw, Joe could see that the muddy slope plunged almost straight down to a tree-filled ravine several hundred feet below.

"Wow," Frank said from the backseat. "There's barely room for two cars to pass on this road."

Joe was the first to spot the car approaching from the opposite direction. "That guy better slow down," he muttered angrily, just as the car disappeared around a bend in the road.

Mingma steered the rickshaw closer to the edge to give the car room to pass them. Joe's eyes were riveted on the steep drop just inches to their right.

Joe sucked in his breath as the oncoming car suddenly reappeared, careening toward them at full speed. There was no room to maneuver and no time to stop.

"Watch out!" Mingma called. They might just make it but with only inches to spare.

Shooting past them, the car clipped their rear wheel. The rickshaw spun out of control and headed straight for the precipice.

Chapter
5

MINGMA TURNED THE WHEEL HARD, trying to bring the rickshaw under control. It was no use. They were skidding along the edge, and in another second they would go over.

"Jump!" Mingma shouted, diving out on the driver's side. Frank hesitated, watching his brother in horror.

Joe was trapped. He struggled to get to the driver's side so he could dive out after Mingma, but there was little room for him to maneuver in in the lurching rickshaw.

Joe heard Frank yell, "Joe!" He wanted to tell his brother to get out, to save himself, but there was no time. Joe felt weightless as the rickshaw flew over the edge. He spotted tree branches

41

right below him. It was a slim chance, but it was the only one he had. He hurled himself clear of the rickshaw.

After that he wasn't quite sure what happened. He fell for a moment, glanced off something solid, saw something green, and grabbed at a branch. He lost his grip, fell again, glanced off another branch, but this time managed to grab hold.

Frank had leaped clear just as the rickshaw went over the cliff, and he immediately made his way back to the edge of the cliff. Aside from a lone tree just below them, the slope was bare all the way down to the ravine.

He cupped his hands and yelled, "Joe!"

"Over here." Joe's voice sounded weak but surprisingly close.

"Are you all right?" Mingma shouted, standing beside Frank.

"I think so." Joe panted. "I got banged up pretty good, but I'm safe. I'm in the tree twenty feet below you."

"If you can get out of the tree," Mingma said, "you should be able to make it back up to us."

"Give me a minute to catch my breath," he said. "I feel a little like your monkey friend Gurkha. But I could use a pair of those big, hairy arms right about now."

Fifteen minutes later Joe had climbed out of his tree and, using rocks and bushes for handholds, scrambled back up the slope to the road. "Sorry about your rickshaw," he said to Mingma, gazing down at the shattered remains.

"At least we're all alive," Mingma answered, glancing up the road in the direction the car had gone. "I'd like to get my hands on whoever was driving that car."

At the moment, there were no cars in sight in either direction. "Looks like we'll have to walk back to Kathmandu," Frank said.

After an hour or so, a passing truck offered them a ride, and they gratefully crawled into the back. Within half an hour, the truck dropped them in downtown Kathmandu.

Mingma was nervous as they arrived at his home. "I have a feeling my father won't take this well," he said. "You'd better wait down here." Ten minutes later Mingma's father came downstairs.

"I am very sorry," he said, "but I think it is best if you return home on the next available flight."

Joe started to protest, but Mingma's father put up a hand. "I am responsible for your safety, and I cannot allow you to be put in any more danger." He turned and climbed back up the stairs.

Joe was beside himself. "He can't make us leave now," he fumed. "Mingma and Pasang need our help. We can't just abandon them."

"We won't," Frank said. "Let's just stay calm.

43

It's a good bet that we won't be able to get a flight for several days. That'll buy us time."

That evening the three friends sat in Mingma's room. While Frank read a book on mountaineering and Mingma stared out the window, Joe paced back and forth. "How can you guys just sit there?" he said.

Frank rolled his eyes. "If you can't entertain yourself, maybe Gurkha the monkey would let you have a rematch."

Mingma turned to Joe. "You told me you might be able to fix my uncle's watch. Want to try?"

Joe agreed, glad for something to do. Frank and Mingma watched as he pried open the casing using a small set of tools. "I'll bet this is the problem right here," he said, pointing. "There's something lodged between the gears."

Using tweezers, Joe pried the object loose. It was a tiny piece of tightly folded paper. "I wonder how this got in there."

"Let me see that," Frank said, unfolding the paper. Two words were written on it: *Kimrong* and *Bimbahadur*.

"Wait a second, Mingma," Joe said excitedly. "Your uncle said that you'd know where to find him when the time was right."

" 'When the time was right,' " Mingma repeated.

"We opened up the watch to make the time right," Joe said. "Pasang left us a message."

Mingma examined the paper. "This looks like my uncle's handwriting," he said. "Kimrong is the name of a village not far from the base of Yeti's Tower. I presume Bimbahadur is a person's name."

"But why all the secrecy?" Joe asked. "If Pasang wanted you to know where he was going, why didn't he just tell you?"

"Maybe he didn't want to be followed," suggested Frank. "At least, not yet."

"Well, like it or not, I say we go after him," Joe declared. "When's the next bus for Kimrong?"

"There is no bus," Mingma said. "There are no roads. The only way to get there is by walking."

"Walking?" Joe said. "How far?"

"Many days."

Joe groaned. "I was afraid of that."

Mingma explained that although there were many villages in the mountains of Nepal, there were almost no roads or other modern amenities beyond Kathmandu Valley. Many of the trails were too rough for even a horse or donkey, so all travel had to be on foot.

"We could fly to Jumla," Mingma suggested. "From there it is only a day or two to walk to Kimrong." He abruptly stopped and shook his head. "But you two are supposed to be heading back to Bayport."

"We can't go back now that we have a lead," Joe said. "We have to go after your uncle."

Mingma didn't answer, and the Hardys said nothing more. They didn't want to force Mingma to disobey his father, but every nerve in their bodies told them that they should catch the next plane for Jumla.

Before they went to sleep that night, Mingma carefully placed his uncle's watch in his dresser. Joe hadn't quite put it back together yet.

After rising early the next morning, they headed to the travel agent as agreed, although Frank and Joe were determined to book tickets to Jumla rather than back to the United States.

The travel agency was located on Durbar Marg, one of Kathmandu's main streets. A man waved them up to the counter as they entered, and Mingma asked about the next available seats to the United States.

The agent tapped the keys on his computer. "The next flight is Thursday. Shall I make a booking?"

"That gives us only two days," Joe complained.

Frank stalled for time. "Will these seats still be available tomorrow?"

"Perhaps," the agent replied. "Perhaps not."

At Mingma's insistence, they made a reservation. "I can hold the seats for twenty-four hours," the agent explained. "If you don't confirm by then, the reservation will be canceled."

As they were about to leave, Mingma turned and asked something else in Nepali. The Hardys heard him mention Jumla.

Back on the street, Joe turned to Mingma. "What did the agent say when you asked about flights to Jumla?"

"He said to try Nepal Airlines."

The Nepal Airlines ticket office was jammed with tourists and locals when they arrived. They were directed to pick a number and take their place in line. Hopeful travelers were called to the counter one by one, but it didn't look like many of them were getting tickets.

Finally, their number was called. A slender woman smiled at them as they walked up to the counter.

"Hello," Frank began. "When is the next available flight to Jumla?"

"All of the flights for this week are full," the woman said, still smiling. "I can put you on a list for next week, but I cannot sell you a ticket."

"Why not?" Joe asked.

"We have a new computer that issues all of the tickets," the woman explained. "Right now the computer is down, so we cannot sell any tickets. Would you like to be on the list?"

"What good will that do?" Frank asked.

The woman shrugged happily. "You may get a ticket when the computer is fixed."

"When will that be?" Joe asked.

"Hard to say. Maybe after one hour, maybe after one week."

They left the ticket office, frustrated. On the way home, Mingma seemed increasingly determined that the Hardys should return to Bayport.

"My father is right," he said. "This is a family problem. I can't risk putting you two in danger."

"And we can't abandon a friend who's in trouble," Frank responded.

Mingma pushed open the front door. The house was strangely silent as he led the way in.

"Hello?" Mingma called out. "Is anyone home?"

"Back here, quick," Mingma's mother said.

Mingma dashed around the corner, the Hardys on his heels. What Joe saw when he stepped into the room stopped him in his tracks.

Mingma's mother was bent over her husband, who lay stretched out on the floor in a pool of blood.

Chapter

6

IT WAS A GRIM SCENE. Ama Sundeki cradled her husband's head in her lap, his blood covering her apron. Mingma dashed toward his stricken father.

"Call a doctor," Mingma's mother said to him. "Somebody broke in upstairs," she told the Hardys. "I think they are gone."

Frank and Joe quickly confirmed that the upstairs was empty. Returning with antiseptic and bandages, they helped Ama Sundeki bandage the wound.

By the time the doctor arrived, Mingma's father was fully conscious. The doctor examined him and declared that he should make a full recovery.

"Your father and I returned home from a visit

to Pasang's family," she said. "We heard noises upstairs, and your father went up, thinking it was you three. Then I saw him struggling with someone in the upstairs hallway. He fell down the stairs and hit his head."

"Did you see the attacker?" Frank asked.

She shook her head. "Whoever it was ran away immediately. They must have gone out a window."

Joe went outside to check for any signs of the attacker while Frank and Mingma went back upstairs. Mingma's room was in total disarray. Drawers and boxes had been overturned. The contents of the closet had been emptied onto the floor.

As they came back down, there was a loud knock on the door. It was Lieutenant Tamang. "We had a call that there was a break-in," he said.

Mingma nodded. "I'm the one who called. Somebody broke in and attacked my father."

Several more police officers entered through the front door, with Joe in tow. "We caught him hiding in back," they reported to Tamang.

"I wasn't hiding," Joe retorted. "I was looking for clues."

"Was anything stolen?" Tamang asked.

"We're not sure yet, but we don't think so," Mingma answered.

"So the intruder was not a thief," Tamang mused. "Then what did he want?" He continued

50

without waiting for them to answer. "Your uncle Pasang is a fugitive from the law. Perhaps he returned for something, and there was a family quarrel."

Mingma was obviously furious about this, but it was his mother who answered. "Someone came in and attacked my husband," she said angrily. "Are you here to protect us or to accuse us?"

Tamang said nothing for several moments. "We will continue our investigation," he said finally. "Good afternoon."

Mingma was dejected after the police left. "My family is in danger, and the police won't help," he moaned. "How can I even think about going after my uncle when—"

Mingma jumped to his feet. "My uncle's watch!" The Hardys followed as he ran up to his room and shuffled through the piles on the floor. "It's got to be here," he said, panic in his voice. They helped him search but found nothing.

"What about the note from your uncle?" Joe asked.

"Gone, too," Mingma said. "That means my uncle is in even more danger."

Frank put his hand on Mingma's shoulder. "At least it means your parents are safe."

Mingma looked at him. "What do you mean?"

Frank explained his reasoning. "Both times there was a break-in, the intruder looked in your room first. Now, the watch is the only thing that's missing. That must have been what he wanted all along. Now that he has it, it's a good bet he won't come back."

"That could also explain why Frank's watch disappeared the night you were attacked," Joe added. "I'll bet whoever it was mistook Frank's watch for your uncle's."

"But you and Joe were the only ones who even knew I had my uncle's watch," said Mingma.

"Your uncle gave you the watch outside Swain's lecture," Frank pointed out. "Right after you left, I saw two other men go out the same door."

"I didn't notice anyone following us," Mingma said. "But it doesn't matter. I have to go to Kimrong to warn my uncle."

"Frank and I should go instead," Joe suggested. "If you left, your parents would be worried sick about you. If we go, your parents won't even have to know. We're supposed to be going home to Bayport anyway."

Mingma looked doubtful. "All right," he said finally. "But I'm going with you."

They all went off to bed, vowing to make another attempt to buy airplane tickets to Jumla in the morning.

The first sound Joe heard the next morning was Frank's voice. "Joe, Mingma's gone," he whispered, shaking his brother awake.

Joe opened one eye, then the other. "What do you mean?"

Frank handed Joe a slip of paper with Mingma's handwriting:

Frank and Joe,
I have put you in too much danger already.
Thanks for everything.

Mingma

Joe groaned. "He picks a time like this to try to be a hero."

Just then there was a knock on the door. It was Mingma's mother, plainly surprised to find the Hardys alone. "Where is Mingma?" she asked.

Joe tried to think of a good answer but couldn't. Reluctantly, he handed her Mingma's note. Considering everything that had happened, he thought she took it pretty well.

"What does this mean?" she asked."Where has my son gone?"

Frank and Joe hesitated, not sure how much to tell her. "We aren't exactly sure where Mingma is," Frank answered, half truthfully. "But we'll find him. We promise."

The Hardys went downstairs to the storage room, and, as they expected, Mingma's backpack and climbing equipment were missing.

"Any question that Mingma is on his way to Kimrong?" Joe asked.

"If we head for the airport right now, maybe we can still catch him," Frank replied.

The Hardys hurriedly gathered their gear. They bid goodbye to Mingma's mother, saying they were not sure when they would return.

"Please bring my son home," she said. "I must stay here to take care of my husband, and I have nobody else to turn to. I know that the police will do nothing."

Hopping a cab, the Hardys headed for Tribhavan Airport. There was surprisingly little commotion there when they arrived. Seeing no sign of Mingma, they asked about flights to Jumla.

"Today's flight has already left," the man behind the Nepal Airlines desk told them. "The Jumla flight always departs first thing in the morning."

"Can we buy a ticket for tomorrow?" Joe asked.

"The flight is always sold out," the man answered. "Your only chance is to go to the gate tomorrow morning and hope that someone does not show up."

They thanked the man and left.

"I hate to lose another day here," Joe said, "but it looks like we don't have any choice."

Frank had an idea. "As long as we're here,

let's pay another visit to the Ministry of Tourism."

Mingma's friend Pertemba was surprised to see the Hardys. Gambling that they could trust him, Frank and Joe told him the full story of Mingma's disappearance.

"Mingma asked you for information about the Waldmann expedition," Joe said. "Were you able to find out anything?"

Pertemba presented them with a large folder, filled with the official accounts of the tragic expedition. Much of the information was new to the Hardys.

"It sounds like a nightmare," Joe commented as he flipped through the records. "The avalanche was on May thirty-first, but the three survivors didn't make it back to Jumla until mid-June. They stumbled around for weeks, with almost no supplies."

"That's strange," Frank said, holding up another paper. "This record shows that at least one of the survivors was evacuated back to Kathmandu from the base of Yeti's Tower on June fourth."

"If the three of them didn't make it to Jumla until the middle of June, how could one of them already have been evacuated on the fourth?"

Pertemba had no explanation. "It is possible there is an error in the records." He shrugged.

The Hardys thanked him. "Be sure to bring Mingma back to us safely," he told them as they left.

The Hardys checked into a hotel near the airport, requesting a 4:00 A.M. wakeup call. The airport was already bustling when they arrived the next morning to join a long line of passengers waiting to check in.

"Ticket, please." The man behind the counter didn't bother to look up at them when it was their turn.

"We don't have any," Frank said. "You see, when we went to the ticket office, the computer wasn't working."

"Today's flight is overbooked. No ticket, no boarding pass."

"Look, we're desperate—" Frank started to say.

The man scowled. "Next."

Joe walked up to another official, who was collecting boarding passes from people as they climbed onto the plane. Joe waited until the stream of passengers had thinned, then approached the man.

"Maybe you can help me," he said quietly. "My brother and I need to get to Jumla today." He pulled out his wallet and opened it, flashing several twenty-dollar bills and making sure the official got a good look.

The man sized him up for a moment, then

`beckoned them to follow him into a small office nearby. "I can get you space on a cargo plane," he told him. "You will have to ride in back with the baggage, and the price will be considerable." He named a figure.

"We'll take it," Joe said. He pulled out several of the twenties and handed them to the man, who led them out through the terminal to a cargo hangar one hundred yards away.

Joe almost reconsidered when he saw the plane. "Do they really expect us to fly in that?" he asked. The plane was a twin-propeller model at least thirty-five years old, badly in need of a paint job, if not a complete rebuild.

"Wow," Frank said, stepping back and admiring the plane. "I've never actually seen one of these. Do you realize what this is, Joe?"

"A dangerous heap of junk."

"This, Joe," Frank said, "is a Y-Eight, the Chinese version of the Russian Antonov Fourteen, or AN-Fourteen for short. Note the tadpole-shaped fuselage with the only door in the back. A real workhorse. The first ones were built in the late fifties. I'm sure it's fine," Frank answered, approaching the pilot. "I assume this aircraft gets regular maintenance."

"Of course." The pilot nodded. "Maintenance is taken very seriously. In fact, the chief mechanic was recently fired for not doing his job properly."

"How's the new chief mechanic?" Joe asked.

"We haven't hired one yet. If you don't want to miss this flight, you had better get in now," the pilot said, collecting his fee from the first man.

Despite their misgivings, the Hardys climbed into the plane and settled into the cargo area, stretched out over large sacks filled with beans and rice. Ahead, they could see the pilot through a narrow doorway that led into the cockpit. After running through his checklist, the pilot fired up the engines, had a brief exchange with the control tower, and taxied out to the end of the runway.

"Prepare for takeoff!" the pilot called to them. The noise of the propellers filled their ears as the plane rattled down the runway and lurched into the air.

"This is the last time I fly in the economy section," Frank quipped. Joe didn't answer but kept his eyes glued to the back of the pilot's head.

They had been in the air for about an hour when the ride began to get bumpy. With every lurch, the plane groaned and rattled. As the jolts become more and more violent, Frank and Joe crawled forward to look out the front window. Clouds had almost totally obscured the view.

"Bad weather," yelled the pilot. "Perhaps we should return to Kathmandu." Instead, he put the plane into a gradual climb to get above the weather.

Frank and Joe just stared out the window at the clouds. A minute later Frank thought he caught a glimpse of ice and snow among the dizzying white and gray cloud formations.

Suddenly, the plane broke free of the clouds, and they were in bright sunlight. Staring ahead, Frank and Joe suppressed a gasp.

A huge ridge of ice and snow loomed directly in front of them, so close that they could clearly see the masses of bluish white ice that hung from the clefts and gorges scarring the face of the rock. The mountain entirely filled their view. It would be impossible to turn the plane in time. They were going to crash.

Chapter
7

FRANK AND JOE WATCHED open-mouthed as the ridge loomed closer. The view was terrifying and breathtaking at the same time. They were gaining altitude but not fast enough. In less than a minute, the plane would be dashed to bits against the jagged, ice-covered rocks along the top of the ridge.

Sucking in his breath, the pilot reached down and jammed both throttle levers wide open. He pulled the yoke up and to the left. The engines screamed as the plane strained to climb through the thin air. The rattling inside the cockpit was deafening, but they were still climbing.

Moments later the plane cleared the steep face by what seemed no more than fifteen feet. Looking down, they could see an icy dropoff of at least five thousand feet, the face of the cliff glistening in the morning sun.

Joe's heart was pounding in his chest. "That was too close," he said.

"Close, but not as close as you think," the pilot said. "You just don't know how big the mountain is."

Joe realized the pilot was right. The ridge was still beneath them, and their progress along it was slower than he would have expected. A sea of clouds stretched into the distance, with great peaks poking up like islands.

"What's that mountain?" Joe asked, pointing to an especially large peak.

"That is Annapurna," the pilot answered. "One of the greatest mountains in Nepal."

Joe remembered seeing Annapurna from Nagarkot. Then it had been more than a hundred miles away. From up close, he could trace the sharp ridges that ran down from the summit. The summit glistened white with snow, but in other sections bare rock was exposed, revealing numerous chasms and ledges.

Half an hour later, they landed safely in Jumla. The town was at the bottom of a large valley. As they approached the runway, Frank and Joe could see that the valley floor was covered with rice paddies.

"When you go through the airport, the police

will check your passports and trekking permits," the pilot told them. "Don't worry, this is routine."

The Hardys thanked the pilot for delivering them safely, scrambled out of the plane, and went into the terminal, where they were directed to a uniformed man sitting behind a table.

"Remember that a trekking permit does not allow you to do any climbing," the man said. He eyed the ice axes and other gear that protruded from their packs.

Frank winked at the man and leaned over the table to whisper. "We just carry this stuff so that my brother can take pictures and impress his friends back home," he said in a low voice. "He wants everybody to think we're big-time mountaineers. But don't worry. I won't let him get anywhere near a real peak."

"What did you tell him?" Joe asked as they left the airport. "That was a funny look he gave me."

"Never mind," Frank said. "It got us out of there, didn't it?"

From the airport it was a short walk to the town. A few shops, along with several restaurants and a small hotel, lined the stone-paved main street. The flight had taken less than two hours, but Frank and Joe had the feeling that they had traveled back through time. Kathmandu, exotic as it was, was filled with cars, lights, and the bustle of the modern world. Here the twentieth century had not arrived.

Frank looked around. "No cars," he said. "No modern roads. Aside from flying, the only way back is to walk."

"How far to the nearest highway?" Joe wondered.

Frank pulled out a map he had picked up in Kathmandu. "I'd say about sixty miles. In this country, that would be a ten-day walk."

"Even the buildings look different from those in Kathmandu," Joe noted, indicating several flat-roofed stone houses. Logs leaning up against the outside of the buildings obviously served as stairways from one level to another.

"That's the Tibetan influence," Frank said. "Tibet is just over the mountains from here."

"Do Tibetans make pizza?" Joe asked. "I'm starving."

They stepped into a restaurant, where an elderly woman greeted them. She didn't answer when they asked for menus, just nodded and vanished into the back after Joe gestured toward his mouth.

A few minutes later, a teenage girl returned, carrying plates piled high with food. "This is *dhal bhat tarkaari*," she announced. "Enjoy."

Joe's heart sank as he looked at his plate. A huge mass of white rice was topped by a few scrawny vegetables in a thin sauce. Knowing that the girl was watching him, he took a large mouthful and pretended to eat with relish.

"Can you tell us how to get to Kimrong?" Frank asked. The girl told them where to pick up the trail just outside town.

"How long does it take?" Joe asked.

"Half a day," she answered. "Or, as we say, one meal."

"Chet would fit right in here." Frank laughed. "A culture where they measure distance by how many meals you have to eat."

"If you are going into the mountains, you should bring as much food as you can carry," the girl told them. "It can be scarce."

The Hardys finished their meal, paid their bill, thanked the girl for her advice, and left. They stopped in a shop to buy supplies. Inside, they found rice and potatoes plus a few canned goods.

"Slim pickings," Joe said. "Good thing we brought all those dehydrated trail foods and stuff from Bayport." He and Frank bought as many cans of potatoes as they could carry and headed for the outskirts of town. Small children waved as they filed past rice paddies.

They found the trail just where the girl had said it would be. Leaving the rice paddies behind, they moved through tall grass and across a river. Then the trail began to climb steeply upward.

Within two hours they had passed through several villages, all of which were even tinier than Jumla. Joe wiped the sweat from his brow.

"Up, down, then up again," he complained. "There's not fifty feet of flat ground in this whole country."

Even though the trail went up and down, the Hardys sensed that overall they were gaining altitude. The ground became drier, and the temperature dropped. At each village, the locals waved their arms to confirm that Kimrong was farther down the road.

Late in the afternoon, they crossed a bridge that spanned a wide river and entered a village. Like most of the others, it consisted of a few houses and other buildings. Expecting to be waved on yet again, they were surprised when a woman nodded to confirm that this was Kimrong. She led them to a teahouse down the street.

Exhausted, they threw down their packs and sat at a table out front. Without taking their order, the woman brought them cups of tea, which they accepted gratefully.

"Okay, so this is Kimrong," Joe said. "Where's the bureau of missing persons?"

Frank waved their hostess over. "We're looking for a friend," he told her. "His name is Mingma."

The woman looked at them blankly. "Wish we had a photograph," Joe said.

Frank tried a different tack. "Is there a Bimbahadur here?" he asked, repeating the name written on Pasang's note.

This got a response. "Bimbahadur?" she repeated. The Hardys nodded enthusiastically. She stuck her head out the back door and called to somebody.

A big, jocular man came in through the same door. "I am Bimbahadur," he said. "Welcome to my teahouse."

The Hardys shook his hand, not sure where to begin. "We're looking for a friend of ours named Mingma," Frank said. "He planned to come here to speak with you. Have you seen him?"

Bimbahadur's face clouded. "Your friend has not been here," he said. "Excuse me. I have some work to finish. My wife will serve you dinner. Afterward, we have rooms upstairs for travelers."

With that, he went back out the door. "I'd say we just hit a nerve," Frank said. "Sounds like Mingma's been here."

"Maybe we can find something out from the other villagers," Joe suggested. "Probably best to wait until tomorrow, though. I doubt anybody will welcome strangers at this hour."

It was getting dark. Bimbahadur's wife brought candles to light their table.

"I guess there's no electricity here," Joe said. "Where am I supposed to plug in my vibrating lounge chair?"

By now they both knew what to expect for dinner, and they were hungry enough to eat large helpings of the *dhal bhat tarkaari* brought by their hostess. She then led them upstairs to a small room with several mattresses, bringing two candles from the dinner table.

"I wonder how safe these candles are in a place like this," Frank said after their hostess had left. There were wooden pillars running from ground level all the way up through the roof. "This place would go up like a tinderbox if it caught on fire."

"Well, it better not catch on fire tonight," Joe said through a yawn. "I'm so beat, I'd probably sleep right through it."

"Sleep while you can," Frank said, blowing out the candles. "We may have a long day ahead of us tomorrow." Despite the day's exertions and the warm comfort of his sleeping bag, he lay awake for a long time.

Even after he dozed off, his sleep was interrupted by vivid dreams. In one dream he sat around a campfire with his brother, Mingma, and several strangers. Everything around them was dark. Suddenly, the campfire flames blazed up unexpectedly, and the air in front of them caught fire. They jumped back, the inferno threatening to engulf them.

Frank woke up. He sat up in his sleeping bag, sweat covering his body. The dream had seemed so real. He thought he could smell the smoke from the campfire.

Then he saw a flame lick up through a crack in the floor. Smoke was creeping under the doorway, and the place was heating up fast.

Bimbahadur's teahouse was on fire.

Chapter

8

"JOE, WAKE UP!" Frank prodded his sleeping brother. "We've got to get out of here."

Joe woke up and leaped to his feet in record time. He dashed to the door.

"Don't open it!" Frank said over the crackling of the flames, which was growing louder by the second. Joe reached out to touch the door and jerked his hand back. It was burning hot.

"We can't go that way," Frank said. "Try the window."

Joe yanked the window open and looked out. The ground dropped away on the side of the building. It was at least forty feet—too far to jump.

Joe dug through his backpack. The flames were

licking up all over the floor now; the door itself had just caught fire. Finally, Joe pulled out a length of rope.

Frank tied the rope to one of the rafters. "You first," Joe said. He felt the searing heat on his back as he watched Frank lower himself on the rope. As soon as Frank got to the bottom, Joe tossed out their backpacks and sleeping bags and followed his brother.

By now, most of the building was engulfed in flames. Frank turned to Joe. "Bimbahadur!" he said.

The Hardys wasted no time dashing around to the front of the building. Bimbahadur was standing out front, horror on his face.

"My wife is still inside!" he said, and ran into the burning building.

"Hold on!" Frank yelled, but Bimbahadur had already disappeared into a wall of smoke and flame. A moment later a loud crash came from inside, followed by a cry for help.

"Stay behind me," Frank told Joe. Pulling their shirts over their faces to protect themselves from the smoke, they ran to the doorway. Peering inside, they could make out Bimbahadur lying on the ground, trapped under a beam.

Moving quickly, they went to Bimbahadur and lifted the beam just enough for him to drag himself free. He was struggling to stand up.

"My wife!" he said, coughing and choking on

the smoke. He pointed. Frank now saw her, cornered behind a wall of flames, terror registered on her face.

"You help Bimbahadur!" Frank called to Joe. Spotting an opening in the flames, Frank leaped through to Bimbahadur's wife. He grabbed her hand and dragged her back through the fire. A section of roof crashed down behind them as they ran out on the heels of Joe and Bimbahadur.

After Bimbahadur assured the Hardys that nobody else was inside, they turned their attention to putting out the fire so it would not spread to the other buildings. Villagers appeared carrying buckets and followed Frank and Joe to the river. Soon a line of men, women, and children formed, passing up buckets of water to soak the fire.

By sunrise the last flames had been doused, but the building had burned almost completely to the ground. Joe patted his brother on the shoulder.

"From now on we always carry a smoke alarm," he said. "What woke you up?"

Frank shrugged. "For some reason, I just wasn't sleeping well," he said. "I tossed all night."

Bimbahadur approached the Hardys. "You saved our lives. Without you, my wife and I would have burned to death. Thank you."

"We're just glad that nobody was hurt," Joe said. "Do you have any idea how the fire started?"

Bimbahadur appeared troubled. "I am afraid that maybe I do," he said. "Yesterday, when I told you that your friend had not come here—this was not true." He glanced up at them again. "Your friend did come, the day before yesterday. But I refused to speak with him."

Frank and Joe waited for him to explain.

"For years I have worked as a mountaineering guide," Bimbahadur continued. "Last year, I was hired by an American to go to Yeti's Tower."

"But I thought there hadn't been any expeditions there in the last six years," Joe interrupted. "Not since the Waldmann expedition."

"Not officially," Bimbahadur replied. "But this expedition was secret. There were no records of our journey. Only three of us went: myself, my employer, and another man named Jang Bu. Our purpose was not to climb the mountain but to search for something."

"What was it that you were looking for?" Frank asked.

"I don't know," Bimbahadur answered. "In particular, my employer was interested in searching near the Chomolungma face. This is a steep rock face, high up the mountain. But storms kept us from ever getting anywhere near it."

"Even if you had made it up, what chance would you have had of finding anything?" Joe asked.

"Everything is preserved by the cold," Bimbahadur answered. "Most expeditions follow similar routes. It is very common for climbers to find items left by previous expeditions."

"So common it has become an environmental hazard," Frank said. "In fact, Mount Everest has been described as the world's highest garbage dump."

"In any case," Bimbahadur continued, "we did find a few items of equipment and such, but nothing that satisfied my employer."

"And who was that?" Frank asked.

Bimbahadur shrugged. "He told us to call him Mr. Jack. I think he was American."

"What did 'Mr. Jack' look like?"

Bimbahadur pointed to Joe. "He had hair like yours. And he was big—even bigger than you."

From the description, Frank and Joe realized this could easily have been Roland Swain. They pressed Bimbahadur for more details. "Did he ever go by the name Roland Swain or any other name?" Frank asked.

"No."

"Can you describe anything else about him?"

Bimbahadur looked embarrassed. "I'm sorry, but to us Nepalese, you Westerners all look alike."

"What does this have to do with our friend Mingma?" Frank asked.

"I'm coming to that," Bimbahadur answered.

"A few months ago I met a Sherpa named Gyalt-sen, who had also been to Yeti's Tower."

Frank and Joe recognized this name. Gyaltsen was the third survivor of the Waldmann expedition, along with Pasang and Swain.

"When I learned that Gyaltsen had been to Yeti's Tower six years ago, I told him about the trip I had made," Bimbahadur said.

"I thought you were supposed to keep that secret," Joe said.

"I'm not very good at keeping secrets," Bimbahadur admitted. "I always thought all the secrecy was foolish. Besides, I was curious. I hoped that Gyaltsen might be able to tell me what it was that Mr. Jack was so eager to find."

Bimbahadur continued his story. "Several days ago Gyaltsen returned, along with a man named Pasang."

"You saw Pasang?" Frank asked. "Do you know where he is?"

Bimbahadur nodded. "I thought you would know him. He and Gyaltsen continued on toward Yeti's Tower.

"Then, the day before yesterday, Jang Bu came." Bimbahadur's eyes narrowed. "Jang Bu is a very bad-tempered man. He was very angry. He knew that I had spoken with Gyaltsen and Pasang. He said if I ever spoke to anyone about Yeti's Tower again, I would regret it."

Bimbahadur hung his head. "Shortly after Jang

74

Bu left, your friend Mingma arrived. But I didn't speak with him because of Jang Bu's warning. That's why I lied to you yesterday."

Frank gestured toward the smoldering building. "You believe Jang Bu was responsible for the fire?" he asked.

Bimbahadur nodded. "Yes. Although I never would have guessed that even he could do such a thing. This fire could have destroyed the whole village."

"Do you know where Mingma is now?" Joe asked.

Bimbahadur shook his head. "If you'll excuse me, I must go see to my wife," he said.

"Bimbahadur's story jibes with everything that's happened," Joe said after he left. "Remember that Gyaltsen visited Pasang just before Swain's lecture. He must have told Bimbahadur's story to Pasang. That explains why Pasang was so upset when he showed up at the lecture. By then he knew about Swain's secret trip."

"He knew about somebody's secret trip," Frank said. "We still don't know for sure it was Swain."

"That's true," Joe conceded, "but the description sure fits." He changed the subject. "So what do we do now?"

"We go on to Yeti's Tower," Frank answered. "It doesn't take a genius to figure out that that's where Mingma headed, following his uncle."

"Unless something happened to him."

After a quick breakfast with the villagers, Frank and Joe struck out in the direction of Yeti's Tower. Bimbahadur thanked them again for saving his family and wished them luck.

Joe was struck by the changes in the country from one day to the next. The Jumla Valley had been filled with rice paddies, but now the brothers were in a much drier region of pine forests.

"We could be somewhere in Colorado," he commented.

After several hours they met a group of Nepalese porters coming in the opposite direction. The Hardys questioned them, hoping for news of Mingma.

One of the porters spoke English. "We saw your friend. He goes to Yeti Himal," he said, using the Nepali word for *mountain*. "I tell him no go."

"Why not?" Frank asked.

"We come from there. This mountain is bad luck. Too many bad accidents. Mr. Swain is very angry. But we think maybe the yeti is more angry."

"Mr. Swain? You mean Roland Swain, the mountain climber?"

"Yes. Mr. Swain pays many rupees. But now we go. Too much bad luck."

Without another word, the porters vanished down the trail. The Hardys continued on. The air was getting colder, and there were more patches of snow. They left the pine forest behind, and the trail gradually narrowed to a thin ledge, with a steep cliff above and a sheer dropoff below.

A wave of dizziness hit Frank as he looked down. The valley floor yawned up from almost a thousand feet below. If one of them fell, he would have nothing to grab. Taking a step, he nearly slipped on loose rock.

"I don't like this," he muttered to himself. "One slip, and we're goners."

Behind him, Joe was also uneasy. He kept his eyes glued on the trail ahead to avoid any misstep, but he couldn't shake the feeling that they were being followed. Several times he turned, thinking he had heard something, but there was nobody in sight behind them.

Then he heard a noise above and caught a glimpse of something falling. It was a rock headed straight for Frank's head.

"Frank!" he called, but it was too late. The rock struck his brother, who crumpled to his knees, dangerously close to the edge.

Joe darted forward, pulling his brother away from the side of the cliff. "You all right?" he asked. Frank didn't answer.

Then Joe heard another noise above him. His heart froze when he looked up. There was a huge boulder hurtling straight toward them.

Chapter
9

JOE WRAPPED HIS ARMS around his semiconscious brother and dove forward. The boulder slammed into the spot where they had been a moment before, missing them by inches.

Joe tumbled over Frank, and his momentum carried him right off the edge of the cliff. He managed to hook his arm around a rock outcropping just as his legs swung out over the abyss.

Joe felt himself slipping, dragged down by the weight of his pack. For a moment, he struggled to pull himself back up, but then he recalled what Pasang had taught him: Rather than trying to pull yourself up onto a ledge, walk your feet up the rock and then press down with your hands to push yourself up. It worked.

Back on the ledge, Joe tried to revive his brother, who was slowly coming around. "Frank, are you okay?" Joe kept glancing up, expecting more rocks to fall on them.

"I think so," Frank began, "but my—"

Suddenly, Joe clutched his brother's arm. High above them, a white figure rose from behind a rock, stood erect for a moment, then disappeared. He couldn't be sure, but it seemed to him that he had made eye contact with the creature. There was a cold intelligence in the gaze that made a chill run down Joe's spine.

"Did you see that?" Joe asked. "I just saw—" He stopped himself, seeing his brother's blank expression. "Can you move? We've got to get off this ledge before more rocks start falling."

Frank nodded. "That rock caught the back of my neck, but I'll be okay. It wasn't a direct hit."

Once Frank stood up and regained his balance, they moved as quickly as possible along the winding ledge. Joe tried to focus on the trail but kept thinking about the figure he had seen. At any moment, he expected rocks to start showering down on them again.

After several hundred yards, the cliff ended, and the trail turned to cross a wide, gradual slope. They stopped to rest.

"Solid ground on both sides," Frank said as he sat down. "What a relief."

Joe examined the back of his brother's neck.

"You've got an ugly bruise, but it doesn't look too serious," Joe told him. "If you're hurting, I can take some of your heavy gear."

"Thanks," Frank said. "I'm okay."

Joe then broached the subject that was foremost on his mind, even though he felt foolish asking the question. "According to all the stories we've heard, the yeti is supposed to have long white fur, right?"

Frank stared at his brother. "That's one theory. And then there are the people who say it's brown or reddish brown. And the others who say it's as tall as a house, with green eyes."

Joe hesitated before continuing. "I'm serious, Frank. I think I just saw the abominable snowman."

"I thought I was the one who almost got knocked out," Frank responded, staring at his brother. "This thin air must be getting to you."

"Mingma's father said a lot of people take the yeti myth seriously," Joe said defensively. "Even some scientists." His eyes narrowed. "Somebody threw those rocks on us."

"There are rock slides in these mountains all the time," Frank said. "It was just our bad luck to be caught by one."

After Frank had rested awhile, the Hardys continued. They trudged on for several more hours, then stopped again to rest. They were gaining altitude rapidly now. Snow was increasingly common, and trees were few and far between. Ahead, the trail continued upward, toward a barren pass.

"I'm beat," Joe proclaimed, gasping for breath. "Just walking is an effort. I didn't think I was this much out of shape."

"You're feeling the altitude," Frank said. "We must be up around sixteen thousand feet by now."

By the time they reached the pass, they were struggling through knee-deep snow. The sun was low, and a heavily overcast sky kept them from seeing any distance.

Snow began to fall just as they crossed the summit. They walked down a short distance and came to a small, snow-covered plateau, just large enough for their tent.

"I don't think we'll see any more villages at this altitude," Frank said. "We'd better pitch our tent here."

The sun went down soon after, and the temperature plummeted. Inside the tent, the Hardys curled into their sleeping bags for warmth.

"So what do we do once we get to Yeti's Tower?" Joe asked. "March into Swain's camp and arrest him for an illegal expedition?"

"First we find Mingma and Pasang," Frank answered.

"That could be tough," Joe said. "It's a big mountain."

"We haven't exactly been lonely since we've

been in this country," Frank replied. "Somehow I have a feeling that when we get where we're going, someone will be there to meet us."

"Could be." Joe nodded. "Let's try to lay low when we get to the mountain. If we run into Swain's party, I'd rather see them before they see us."

Rolling over, Frank mumbled in agreement. A minute later they were both fast asleep.

It was surprisingly warm and bright inside the tent when Frank awoke the next morning. He had heard that at high altitude, the sun could be amazingly intense. Zipping open the door, he stuck out his head. He froze, struck dumb by the scene in front of him.

"Joe," he said. "Take a look at this."

The clouds had broken to reveal a stunning panorama. They were looking down into a wide valley, the floor of which was covered by a huge glacier. Sheer ridges rose on both sides of the valley. At the far end, a jagged white spike glistened in the morning sun, towering above the surrounding peaks. It was a mountain like none they had ever seen.

"I guess that must be Yeti's Tower," Frank said.

"How could anyone possibly climb that?" Joe asked.

They broke camp quickly and headed down the

slope. The frozen mass of the glacier lay ahead as they approached the valley floor. Frank paused to study the terrain.

"The only way across is to go over the glacier," he said. "We'll have to rope together."

A glacier, Pasang had explained to the Hardys, was like a river of ice. It might flow less than an inch in an entire day, but it flowed. The result was that cracks could open anywhere; a spot that was safe one day might be treacherous the next.

The going was slow, since they had to test the ground with the shaft of their ice axes at each step, but by midafternoon they had crossed most of the valley. As they approached, Yeti's Tower loomed ever higher until it finally blocked out the sun.

Suddenly, Joe grabbed Frank's arm. "Look," he said, keeping his voice low. Ahead, a group of men approached across the rolling icy surface of the glacier. "Let's hide."

Cover was scarce. For lack of a better idea, the brothers threw themselves down behind a bank of snow. Within a couple of minutes, a group of Nepalese porters passed close by, moving quickly.

"Porters abandoning Swain's party?" Frank guessed.

After they had passed, the Hardys waited several minutes, then stood up. They had taken only a few steps in the direction of the mountain when they heard a rough voice behind them.

"Who are you two?" it demanded.

Frank and Joe turned to face three large men. They had thick beards and leathery skin and were fully equipped for mountaineering.

"We're trekkers," Frank said. "We heard there was an expedition to climb Yeti's Tower, and we thought it might be interesting to come and watch."

"This is no place for trekkers," one of the men said, studying them closely. "Especially trekkers who look like they're still in school."

Joe bristled at the man's tone. "Who are you?"

"Call me Hooper. My friends and I are from that expedition you heard about. I suggest you head right back the way you came. We don't have time for baby-sitting."

"You have no right to tell us what to do," Frank responded evenly. "We plan to continue up the valley and camp at this end."

One of the other men spoke up. "If they're going to insist, they might as well come with us. With everything that's happened lately, we're better off having them in camp with us."

"Who's leading your expedition?" Joe asked.

"Roland Swain," came the answer.

An hour later they arrived at Swain's base camp. It was in the shadow of Yeti's Tower, on a section of rock blown free of snow by the wind. A number of large tents had been erected to house men and supplies.

On one side of the camp, a large heap of tattered equipment was piled. "You guys sure make a lot of garbage," Joe said.

"That's equipment left behind by the last expedition six years ago," one the climbers explained. "They also used this site."

Joe scowled. "Kind of like camping on a graveyard," he muttered.

"There are no bodies here," Hooper answered. "If there's a graveyard anywhere, it's up on the mountain."

Frank and Joe were led into a large mess tent. Inside, several men and a dark-haired woman sat around a table. A sandy-haired man sat at the end of the table, wrinkles appearing in his broad forehead as he looked up at them.

The beginnings of a beard had formed since they had seen him giving a lecture in Kathmandu, but Frank and Joe recognized Roland Swain.

"I hear you boys want to tag along with us," he boomed.

"We're very interested in climbing," Frank said. "We wanted to see what we could learn."

Swain gave them a hard look. "Unfortunately, we aren't in a very hospitable mood these days. We've had quite a few unfortunate incidents. One of my men was almost killed yesterday when a rope broke. That was only the latest in a string of problems.

"Some of the locals claim that by coming here,

we have unleashed the wrath of the yeti," Swain continued. His eyes hardened. "My men and I suspect sabotage. So we were a bit perplexed to find you two hiding behind a snowdrift."

Before the Hardys could respond, they heard a commotion outside. Swain and his men stepped quickly out of the tent. Frank and Joe followed. A crowd had gathered in the center of the compound.

"What's going on here?" Swain demanded, making his way to the center of the mob. Joe sucked in his breath as he caught a glimpse of the person at the center of the mob.

It was Mingma. He stood facing one of Swain's porters, who was brandishing an unusually shaped, curved knife, pointing the tip right at Mingma's chest.

Chapter
10

FRANK WANTED TO YELL OUT to their friend but thought better of it. He decided it was best not to do anything to distract him. Instead, moving silently through the crowd, Frank positioned himself behind the angry porter.

Just as the porter lunged at Mingma with his knife, Frank moved to intercept. A single catlike move put him in position to knock the knife out of the man's hand with a perfectly placed karate kick. In the same instant, Joe dove forward to tackle the porter and quickly had him in a wrestling hold.

Then the entire camp burst into action. Frank, Joe, and Mingma were all seized, surrounded, and outnumbered. There was no point in resisting.

"Hold everything!" Swain's booming voice resonated above the fray. His eyes blazed as he glared in turn at Frank, Joe, and then Mingma. "Nobody moves until I get some answers," he said. "Now, who are you three, and what are you doing here?"

It was Mingma who responded, meeting Swain's gaze. "I want to know what you've done with my uncle Pasang," he demanded. "I know that he's here—unless you have murdered him."

Swain stared down at Mingma. "What are you talking about? I presume you mean the same Pasang who attacked me in my room, back in Kathmandu. I haven't done anything to him. Although I would have if I had seen him."

"This man is wearing my uncle's equipment," Mingma shot back, indicating the porter he was fighting with. "That yellow parka was given to my uncle by a French mountaineer. I recognize it. So don't tell me you haven't seen Pasang."

The porter began speaking rapidly in Nepali, gesturing toward the pile of tattered equipment left behind in years past. Another man translated: "He says he found the parka buried in the snow, along with other items of abandoned equipment."

Seeing that the gear did look faded, Frank put his hand on Mingma's shoulder and said, "He could be telling the truth."

Swain had a thoughtful expression on his face. "If Pasang is somewhere in the area, then that explains who has been trying to sabotage us." He scowled at Mingma. "Your uncle must be a real character. First he tries to lodge an ax in my skull, then he sends a bunch of teenagers to spy on my expedition."

"My uncle is innocent," Mingma replied evenly. "He never hurt you or anyone else."

"And we weren't spying," Joe added. "We have as much right to be here as you do."

"You were hiding behind a snowdrift," Swain said, "but we caught you. Let's see how much trouble Pasang makes now that we've got you three as insurance."

Frank sized up Swain's party as they spoke. He counted seven westerners, plus four men he recognized as high-altitude Sherpas by their gear. In addition, there were roughly thirty porters.

Just then somebody called out from the back of the crowd. "Vadim and Kasia are back. They made it to the top of the Chomolungma face."

This news transformed the entire camp. The Hardys and Mingma were forgotten as the throng parted. Two figures limped up to Swain, both on the brink of collapse.

Joe stared at the two climbers. They looked as if they'd spent a week in a deep freeze. Their clothes were covered with frost. Either of them could be the abominable snowman, he thought. Their eyes were gaunt, and patches of skin on their faces were blackened from frostbite.

"The snow last night nearly killed us," one rasped, speaking with a heavy accent, "but we did it." Joe was surprised to see it was a woman as she pulled down her hood.

Swain was clearly excited by this report. "The Chomolungma face at last," he said, forgetting about the Hardys and Mingma. "Did you see anything up there?" The two slowly shook their heads.

Swain said nothing for a moment, then barked several orders to his men. "Someone get these two to first aid. Hooper, Thondup, follow me." Without another word, he started toward his tent.

"What about these three?" Hooper asked him, indicating Mingma and the Hardys.

"Put them in the supply tent," he said, "and make sure they stay there."

Hooper and several others escorted them to a large gray tent piled high with boxes of food and ordered them inside.

"Take off your boots and give them to me," he ordered.

"If you want my boots, you can come get them yourself," Joe said.

"Don't push me," Hooper growled.

For a moment it looked as if there would be trouble. Then Frank interrupted. "Just leave us one pair of boots for trips to the latrine."

"Fair enough," Hooper replied. Joe stood glowering as Frank and Mingma removed their boots and handed them over. Hooper also took their packs and other gear but left them their sleeping bags.

"What's the deal with letting him take your boots?" Joe asked after Hooper left.

"Cool it," Frank told him. "If you pick a fight now, we'll end up tied up or worse. As it is, they'll probably leave us alone for a few hours. This could be our best chance to find out what Swain and his men are up to."

Joe turned to Mingma. "What was that place that Swain was so excited about, the Chomo-something-or-other?"

"The Chomolungma face," Mingma corrected him. "This is probably the main obstacle to climbing Yeti's Tower. It's sheer rock, almost a thousand feet high. People believed it was unclimbable until the Waldmann twins finally made it up, six years ago.

"But they never made it any farther," he continued. "That's where they were killed by the avalanche."

"Bimbahadur also mentioned the Chomolungma face," Frank said. "That's what he said his employer was trying to reach."

Mingma looked at him. "You've spoken with Bimbahadur?"

The Hardys nodded, filling Mingma in on everything that had happened since he'd left Kathmandu. The conversation then returned to the day's events. It was pretty obvious that Swain and Bimbahadur's employer—whether he was Swain or some other westerner—were looking for something on or near the Chomolungma face.

"Is the face near the top of the mountain?" Frank asked.

Mingma shook his head. "From there, it's still several thousand feet to the top, but the route is supposed to be straightforward from that point. The altitude and weather become the main obstacles then. Of course," he added, "nobody knows for sure. Nobody has done it yet."

Within two hours night had fallen. Voices barked orders, and there was plenty of movement outside the tent. It sounded like a large group planned to move out in the morning. Meanwhile, the weather was getting worse. The temperature had dropped, and the tent was buffeted by wind.

"I wish we could see what was going on," Joe said.

A few minutes later the door opened, and Hooper entered the tent, carrying plates of food.

"How long are you going to make us sit here?" Joe asked.

Hooper shrugged. "You should have taken my advice and headed back the other way." He turned to leave. "For your own good, make sure you stay put. If you make a run for it in this weather, you'll wind up dead for sure."

Joe peered out the door after they had finished

eating. "Hooper's right," he said. "Even I wouldn't be crazy enough to go anywhere tonight."

"That doesn't mean we can't do some exploring around here," Frank suggested. "I think I'll take a little walk. If anybody sees me, I'll just say I got lost on the way to the latrine."

Pulling on Joe's boots, Frank stepped out of the tent. Immediately, he was met by a powerful blast of wind and snow. He could barely see three feet in front of him. Ducking his head against the wind, he headed in the direction of the mess tent.

After a few minutes the mess tent came into view, aglow with light. Shadows moved inside. Putting his ear up against the tent, Frank was able to make out voices.

"You're sure you followed the exact route I described?" The voice was Swain's.

It was Kasia who answered. "We had to. It's the only way up. There was no sign of anything."

"It's hard to know what to expect after six years," Swain said. "We'll just have to keep looking."

As he was straining to hear the conversation, Frank felt a hand clamp down on his shoulder. "What are you doing out here?" a voice demanded. Frank whirled around to face two of Swain's men.

"I went out to go to the latrine and couldn't find my way back—" he began.

"Save it," answered one of the men, grabbing Frank's arm and dragging him into the mess tent. Swain, Kasia, Vadim, Hooper, and the Sherpa named Thondup all looked up as they entered. "Look who we caught snooping outside."

"I wasn't snooping," Frank said, deliberately using a whiny voice. "I went out to go to the bathroom and got lost. I couldn't see my own hand in front of my face out there."

Swain scowled. "I don't have time for this," he snapped. "Put him back with the others. And tie them up this time, so they stay put."

Hooper started leading Frank back to the supply tent. "I don't suppose I could grab my insulated camping mattress from my pack," Frank asked him. "The tent floor is ice cold. We could get hypothermia even in our sleeping bags."

Grudgingly, Hooper made his way to a dome-shaped tent opposite the mess tent. He unzipped the door, hauled out their packs one by one, and pulled the camping mattress out of each. Glancing inside, Frank guessed that the tent was normally occupied by two people.

Returning Frank to the supply tent, Hooper brought ropes and bound each of them hand and foot.

"Not too tight," Frank said. "If we lose circulation in this weather, we'll get frostbite for sure."

"You should have thought of that before you

went snooping around," the man retorted. But he didn't tie the ropes very tightly.

Lying in the darkness, Frank told Joe and Mingma about the conversation he had overheard. "I also found out where they're keeping our packs," he finished.

"I wonder what Swain is looking for after all these years," Joe said.

"That's what we have to find out," Frank answered, closing his eyes. But as he lay on his stomach and listened to the fury of the Himalayan storm outside, a suspicion began to form that caused a chill to run up his spine.

Hours later Frank was still lying awake, tugging at the rope that held his wrists together. Morning had not yet arrived, but the wind had died.

"Joe, Mingma, wake up," he whispered. "The storm's breaking, and I've almost got my hands free."

Sitting up, Frank managed to work himself into a position where his brother could untie his hands. A few minutes later they were all loose.

"Let's get out of here," Joe said.

Outside, Frank led them to the dome tent that held their bags. They quietly unzipped the door and opened it, prepared to fight if necessary. But the sleeping inhabitants never stirred.

Hefting their packs, they left the camp and moved north along the base of Yeti's Tower. The mountain's shadow blocked out the moonlight as they trudged through deep snow, straining to put as much distance as possible between themselves and Swain's camp.

Soon the storm picked up again, slowing their progress. Unable to see more than a few feet through the blinding snow, they roped themselves together to avoid being separated.

"Maybe Hooper was right," Mingma said during a rest, hollering over the storm. "We shouldn't have tried to go anywhere in this weather. I doubt we could even find our way back." Frank and Joe didn't answer.

A few minutes later, Mingma clutched Frank's arm and pointed ahead. There was a dim light visible through the gloom. Hurrying toward it, they found themselves standing at the entrance to a lighted cave. They filed in, Mingma in the lead. Frank, who was bringing up the rear, had to stoop to avoid bumping his head on the low roof. As he did, he heard Mingma shout.

Frank looked up and caught a glimpse of his brother struggling with someone.

Then Joe disappeared, and the light went out.

Frank charged forward. He had no idea what he was going after, but he knew he had to try to find his brother. He bent as low as he could, holding his arms up to protect his head.

Then, out of the pitch blackness, somebody jumped on top of him. An arm wrapped around his neck, and a hand pulled on his arm. Frank drove his elbow into his attacker, heard a grunt, and managed to shake himself loose.

Free of his attacker but off balance, Frank tottered backward. On the third step, his foot found nothing but air. His hands reached wildly for something to grip as he fell.

Chapter

11

FRANK FELL BACKWARD in total darkness. For an
instant, he felt the terror of being suspended in
midair. He wondered how long he'd be falling,
then all at once he landed—on somebody.
There was a grunt as he hit, followed by a
familiar groan. A powerful arm locked around
his neck.

"Joe! It's me!" Frank gasped.

Joe relaxed. "Are you all right?"

"I think so." Frank rolled clear of his brother
and pushed himself up onto his knees. "Mingma,
where are you?"

"Over here," came the answer. "What happened?"

"I think we're in some kind of a pit," Joe said.

98

He stood up and started searching with his hands for a way out.

Then a powerful light blinded them from above. "Do not move," someone commanded. The beam swept over Joe, then Frank, settling on Mingma.

"Mingma," said a familiar voice choked with surprise. "Is that you?"

It was Mingma's uncle Pasang.

Pasang threw down a rope, and Mingma and the Hardys climbed out of the pit. Pasang's companion, who was introduced as Gyaltsen, handed them cups of hot tea. They sat down on the rock floor of the cave and sipped the welcome warm liquid.

Pasang sat down beside them. "I am very sorry for your rough reception just now," he said. He turned to Mingma. "I am especially sorry to you. Disappearing so suddenly without any explanation was terrible. But I had to protect our family."

Mingma clutched the cup in his hand. "I didn't want to believe you when you said you were going away. Then, the next morning, the police came, saying that you had tried to kill Swain."

"You know I would never do that," Pasang said. He changed the subject. "How did you find us?"

They related their whole story, beginning with the police visit the morning after Pasang's disappearance. Pasang was particularly concerned about the attack on Mingma's father and their capture and treatment by Swain.

"We were lucky to find you," Mingma said.

Pasang gave them a stern look. "I'm grateful to you for trying to help," he said, "but you should not have come. It is much too dangerous."

"You sound like my father," Mingma protested. "If you didn't want me to come after you, why did you leave the message in the watch?"

"I had to leave some message, in case I never came back," Pasang answered. "I never thought you would find it so quickly."

Mingma shrugged. "I had some help from Joe."

Frank turned to Pasang. "What made it so urgent for you to leave?"

Pasang took a deep breath and said, "Six years ago, when I was blamed for causing the avalanche, it ended my career as a mountaineer. The shame and humiliation were too much for me. Ever since, I have replayed those events of six years ago in my mind.

"Supposedly, the avalanche happened because a rope that I set came loose," he continued. "But I know that I set the rope properly."

"It still could have come loose," Joe said. "Accidents happen."

"That's what I told myself," Pasang agreed. "But I was never convinced. When I learned

Swain had become rich by inheriting the Wald-mann fortune, I became suspicious. Later I learned from Gyaltsen that Swain had made a secret trip to Yeti's Tower."

Frank broke in at this point. "How do you know it was Swain?" he asked. "All Bimbahadur said was that the man who hired him was a big American, with light-colored hair."

"It has to be Swain," Pasang replied. "There is no doubt in my mind. He murdered his step-brothers, and now he's returning to the scene of his crime—the top of the Chomolungma face."

"The Chomolungma face," Joe interrupted. "Two of Swain's party reached it yesterday. Swain was anxious to hear what they found up there."

Pasang and Gyaltsen were agitated by this news. "If Swain's men have already been there, then we have no time to lose," Gyaltsen said. "We have to make it up there ourselves."

"For what?" Frank asked. "What do you hope to find?"

"To press a murder charge," he said, "you need physical evidence. A body, for example."

There was a long silence. Something was still troubling Frank, and he mustered the nerve to ask the question on his mind. "Swain claims that someone has been trying to sabotage his expedi-tion," he began.

Pasang caught Frank's drift immediately. "We

have done nothing to sabotage him," he said vehemently. "We are here to find the truth, not to put more lives in danger."

"Fair enough," Joe said. "Then who is sabotaging his expedition?"

Gyaltsen shrugged. "Perhaps Swain and his men are imagining things. Or perhaps they made up the whole thing as an excuse to keep you prisoners."

"Up here they could have done whatever they wanted with us," Joe muttered. "They didn't need to make up an excuse."

Joe hardly slept that night. The next day they would begin their ascent toward Chomolungma. Pasang and Gyaltsen had told him and Frank what to expect. It would be like no climb they had ever done. They would ascend as far as they could in the morning, carrying equipment to set up an advance camp that they could use as a base for future assaults on the mountain.

Once they set up the advance camp, they would come back to the cave to spend the night. By climbing high during the day and then descending to sleep, they would allow their bodies to adjust to the extreme altitude. Climbers who went too high too fast risked a condition called high-altitude edema. Fluid would build up in either the brain or the lungs, causing death if the victim didn't descend.

Joe finally dozed off, but it seemed as if he slept only a few minutes before Mingma woke him. "What's wrong?" Joe asked. "It's still pitch dark."

"The safest time to cross the snow slopes is just before sunrise," Mingma answered. "When the sun comes up, the snow softens, and the danger of avalanches is greater."

"Avalanches, blizzards, altitude sickness," Joe said. "I'd feel much safer back in Bayport, getting shot at."

"Save your breath," Frank said. "You'll need it."

Frank was right. The Hardys had been warned that they would feel the altitude, but the reality was a surprise. Every step was an effort. Carrying heavy packs through snow and ice drove them to the limits of their strength.

During a brief pause, Joe surveyed their surroundings. This side of the mountain had two main ridges. They were making their way up one of them. The other sloped off toward the northeast. Above them, the two ridges came together to form a horn-shaped summit.

"From here, the top doesn't look so far off," Joe commented.

"That's not the real summit you're looking at," Gyaltsen told him. "That's just a foothill. Beyond that horn is the Chomolungma face, which leads to the real summit, thousands of feet above."

They continued along the ridge until it narrowed to a knife-edge. Then they descended from the ridge and began to move along a glacier.

After an hour they had almost reached the top of the glacier. In front of them, an enormous crack split the glacier almost in two. The crack ran horizontally, right across their path.

Pasang explained that this was a special type of crevasse, called a *bergschrund*, that formed near the top of a glacier. "Remember that a glacier is like a river of ice. The *bergschrund* forms at the origin, right where the glacier pulls away from the icecap," he explained.

They moved sideways across the crevasse, looking for a way across. Eventually, they came to a spot where an ice bridge spanned the gap. The Hardys watched as Pasang made his way carefully across, testing each step with the shaft of his ice axe. From a safe distance, Gyaltsen worked the rope to support him in case of a fall.

Pasang was almost all the way across when they heard a loud crack. Pasang dove for the far side, burying the pick of his axe in the snow to save himself from being dragged down as the bridge crumbled behind him.

"So much for the ice bridge," he called back, panting. He caught his breath, and within minutes, he and Gyaltsen had set up a rope ladder across the gap. Soon they were all across.

They struggled upward for another hour until

they came to a sheltered spot along the ridge. Pasang turned to Frank, Joe, and Mingma. "We will set up the advance camp here," he said. "After a rest, the three of you will go back to the cave. Gyaltsen and I will continue up."

Joe was obviously disappointed. "Do we have to?" he asked. "How about we just rest for an hour?"

Gyaltsen shook his head. "Your spirit is admirable," he said. "But you have come too high, too fast. The altitude can kill the strong just as easily as the weak."

Joe had to admit that his heart was still throbbing wildly in his chest even though they had been resting for several minutes.

Pasang and Gyaltsen took a brief rest, then struck out. Frank, Joe, and Mingma watched them climb upward along the ridge until they disappeared.

"They make it look so easy," Joe commented.

"They have spent most of their lives in these mountains," Mingma said. "Their bodies have had time to adjust. But it is never easy. Climbers who become too confident almost always wind up dead."

The three ate a quick lunch and then headed back. By early afternoon they had made their way back to where the rope ladder bridged the wide crevasse. Mingma crossed first, followed by Frank.

Then Joe started across. As he reached the center of the ladder, he heard a *twang*, and the ladder gave way underneath his right hand and foot. He scrambled for a grip as his body lurched suddenly to one side.

Joe was dangling precariously above the crevasse, his arms clutching the half-broken ladder. Only a single rope saved him from disaster.

There was another *twang*, and a shock went through the rope that echoed in the pit of Joe's stomach. For a moment the rope held. Hardly daring to breathe, he threw off his backpack to reduce the weight on the rope.

Then he heard a final, sickening *twang* as the last rope snapped.

Chapter

12

FRANK AND MINGMA HEARD the last two snaps
of the rope ladder. They also saw it separate at
their end, right in front of them.

They watched in horror as Joe fell away from
them. Still clinging to what remained of the ladder, he swung like a pendulum toward the far
wall of the crevasse. Then he struck the wall with
a thud, lost his grip, and disappeared into the
icy depths.

Joe thought it was all over. The crevasse was
filled with an eerie blue light that faded into
darkness as he fell. He couldn't help wondering
how long it would be until he slammed into the
ground.

When the impact came, it felt more like skidding into first base. Rather than hitting bottom, he had merged with the ice wall as it curved up underneath him. His free fall had turned into an uncontrollable slide.

Out of control, he guessed he must be sliding along the bottom of the crevasse. It was like some wild ride in a frozen amusement park. He managed to get himself into a sitting position, sliding feet first.

He couldn't tell how far he had slid before a crack of light became visible. Then, suddenly, he was in daylight again, falling through open air, until he landed in a mass of whiteness, gasping for air as more snow came crashing down on him. He was engulfed in darkness once more.

Frank and Mingma leaned forward over the edge of the crevasse as far as they dared, peering into the icy depths.

"Joe!" Frank yelled. There was no answer. "Help me anchor a rope," Frank said to Mingma. "I'm going in after him."

Lowering himself into the crevasse, Frank couldn't help but notice the cool, eerie beauty of the place. As he went deeper, he felt the ice close in around him. It was silent inside, deathly silent, he couldn't help thinking, as he came to the end of his rope.

He called out his brother's name over and over, but there was no answer.

Below him, the walls closed in, then curved out of sight. He wouldn't allow himself to imagine his brother trapped in the depths below, swallowed up in an icy grave.

Joe's lungs screamed for air as he struggled to dig himself out of the snow. He had landed hard, and the impact had knocked the wind out of him. He was completely buried in snow, but he could sense the light above.

Mustering his strength, he managed to dig upward. After several minutes of hard effort, he punched through to the surface. For a moment, he sat gasping, his lungs greedy for air, then he pulled himself free of the snowbank.

He winced as he stood up. He felt as if he had been run over by a herd of yaks, but at least all of his limbs seemed to be working.

"Thanks for the ride, but next time I think I'll walk," he said out loud, speaking to the snowdrift.

The crevasse had spit him out into a snowfilled chute. Looking down the length of the chute, Joe saw a rock outcrop jutting up on the right. On the left, a steep wall climbed upward toward the massive rock formation that Pasang had called the northeast ridge.

He looked back at the mass of the glacier behind him but didn't waste his breath yelling for help. He knew he had slid too far to be within earshot of his companions.

He also knew that without any of his gear, he would never be able to make his way back up the glacier. He started down toward the rocks on the right side of the chute. The snow formed a perfect white surface that stretched out below him.

Then he saw the footprints.

Frank had dropped as far as he could into the crevasse. Hanging from the end of the rope, he saw no sign of Joe. He peered down to where the icy walls curved out of sight. Somewhere down at the bottom, there was a source of light.

Frank made his way back up the rope to where Mingma waited. "No sign of Joe," Frank said. "But I could see light at the end. He may have come out of the crevasse somewhere to the north of us."

"I don't understand what happened," Mingma said. "That ladder never should have broken."

Frank helped him haul up the remains of the rope ladder that still hung down in the crevasse. Examining the breaks, they could see that the ropes had been partially cut.

Frank's eyes blazed. "One way or the other, we'll find out who did this."

They roped themselves together and made

their way north along the crevasse, keeping a safe distance from the rim. After about half a mile, Mingma pointed up toward the northeast ridge. "There's someone moving up there," he said.

Frank took out his binoculars. He could make out a tiny figure, walking erect. "Joe couldn't possibly have made it up there so quickly," he said. "That must be one of Swain's men."

Mingma was puzzled. "I thought Swain's men were all busy trying to climb the mountain from the other side," he said.

"It is strange," Frank agreed. "But we can't worry about it right now. We have to find Joe."

The next hour brought them no luck. After some distance, the crevasse split. While the main seam continued north, the side split forced them to head down the mountain.

Mingma led the way down, looking for a way across, but the gap widened as they went. Then Mingma stopped.

"We can't go any farther in this direction," he said as Frank came up beside him.

Frank sucked in his breath as he took in the view. The glacier dropped abruptly in front of them. Huge towers of ice, called seracs, dangled over the precipice. Hundreds of feet below, they could see where other seracs had fallen, shattering when they landed.

Frank had seen waterfalls before, but this was his first icefall. In other circumstances, he would have been awed by the dramatic scene. Right now, he could think only of his brother.

"If Joe managed to get out of the crevasse, it must have been somewhere up there," he said, pointing back up toward the ridge. He clung desperately to the belief that his brother was alive.

"We'll have to backtrack and find a way up," Mingma said. He looked up at the sun, which was already low over the mountains. "We've got to hurry. The day is running out."

Meanwhile, Joe stooped to examine the footprints in the snow. He could clearly make out the imprint of boot soles. Someone had crossed the chute, just below where he stood.

It was obvious that the tracks were fresh. It had snowed the night before, and these footprints weren't even frosted over.

The tracks ended at the base of the steep wall north of him. There were clear signs that the wall had been climbed from that point. Without any gear, though, Joe would be unable to follow. He knew he needed food and equipment to survive.

He decided to follow the tracks down to their source. In this direction the trail led back to the rocky outcrop on the far side of the chute. Joe stayed low as he made his way to the top, hoping to spot anyone moving along the trail before they saw him.

Reaching the top of the rocks, Joe froze. There

was a tent a hundred feet below, sheltered by the very rocks on which he stood.

There was no reason anyone should be camped here. Swain's group was supposed to be off to the south, attacking the mountain from the valley side. Still, Joe was in no position to walk down to the tent and ask the people for their IDs.

He waited a few minutes, hoping to get a look at the camp's inhabitants. There was no sign of life. Finally, he ran out of patience. Making his way down, he strolled right up to the tent.

"Hello," he said. "Mr. Pizza here. Did anyone order a large pepperoni?"

There was no answer. Joe looked around, then unzipped the door of the tent. Inside, he saw the usual camping and climbing gear.

Just as he was about to close the door of the tent again, the gleam of a metal cylinder caught his eye. A second look confirmed his suspicion. He was looking at a high-powered hunting rifle.

He had a bad feeling. He thought this tent shouldn't be here. And he *knew* the rifle shouldn't.

Joe had read that some of the early mountaineering expeditions in Nepal had brought along rifles to use for hunting animals to eat. As far as he knew, that hadn't happened for many years. Besides, Joe knew a little about guns. This wasn't the type of rifle designed for shooting pigeons or rabbits or even deer. This was built to stop a stampeding elephant.

Joe had a sudden desire to get away from the campsite. Stepping outside, he was aware of how cold it had become. He pulled the hood of his jacket close around his face and looked around.

Above him, he saw a figure coming down from the same rocks where he had just been. Joe ducked, ran away from the campsite, and hid behind a snow-covered boulder a short distance away.

The figure moved skillfully over the rough terrain. It was a tall man, Joe guessed, but he couldn't get a good look because the man's face was bundled against the cold. Approaching the campsite, the man walked right past Joe's hiding place and disappeared into the tent.

Joe waited. The hunting rifle had made him wary, but he knew that he couldn't stave off the effects of hunger, cold, and altitude for much longer. Sooner or later he would have to declare himself and hope for the best.

The cold cut through his clothing, chilling him to the bone. Without meaning to, he dozed.

When he woke, the sun was just about to disappear below the mountains. He rubbed the sleep from his eyes, then looked ahead. Thinking that he must still be dreaming, he rubbed his eyes again.

A large, semihuman creature towered in front

of him. It stood erect, human in shape, but its back and shoulders were hunched, giving it an apelike appearance. The long hair that covered the creature's arms and legs shone whitish gray in the late-afternoon light as it moved toward him.

Crouched behind the rock, Joe steeled himself for battle, his mind still unable to accept what his eyes were telling him.

The abominable snowman was walking straight toward him.

Chapter

13

Joe had only a few moments to prepare himself. Despite its hunched back, Joe guessed that the creature stood much taller than he did. Its movements were heavy but sure-footed.

Everything Joe had heard about the fabled yeti of the Himalayas had dealt with the question of whether or not the creature even existed. He had never heard anything about the best strategy to wrestle one.

Stay low, he decided. He crouched, ready to spring for the creature's legs.

But the moment never came. Instead, Joe watched, stunned, as the yeti walked right past him and began making its way back up the same trail that Joe had come down earlier that day.

Only then did Joe notice that the yeti was carrying an ice ax. Joe quickly made his way back to the tent. It was empty, and most of the equipment was still inside—except for the hunting rifle.

Grabbing an ice ax and other supplies, Joe set out in pursuit. He could see the yeti moving swiftly up the rocks ahead of him. He kept his distance and tried to match its pace.

Meanwhile, Frank and Mingma had returned to the spot where Joe originally disappeared. Frank was growing more and more frustrated and concerned. It was almost dark, and there was no sign of Joe. They had walked a great distance along the crevasse, only to hit a dead end above the icefall and be forced to backtrack.

They still hoped to find Joe to the north, but the chasm kept them from moving in that direction.

"I guess we'll have to head south and hope we find a way across the crevasse," Frank said. "Then we'll double back on the opposite side."

Mingma nodded. "We'll have to be careful. It's much more dangerous after dark. Also, we might run into Swain's party in that direction."

"I'd even be glad to see them, if they can help us find Joe."

An hour after they set out, it was dark. The moon was just coming into view over the ridge. They had come to the end of the glacier without finding a way across the crevasse. A large buttress of rock now blocked their way. The opposite wall of the crevasse came up against the same rock.

"If we head up into these rocks, we should be able to work our way along and come down on the far side of the crevasse," Mingma suggested.

A few minutes later, they were scrambling among the rocks. Mingma pointed upward. "That ledge looks like it runs in the right direction," he said. "If only we can get up to it."

Frank was about to answer when they heard a gruff voice behind them. "All right, freeze!"

Frank froze, then turned slowly, ready to hit the ground—or start swinging with his fists—if necessary. Beside him, Mingma did the same.

Frank recognized Roland Swain, along with Hooper, Vadim, and several others, staring up at them. They were fully dressed in expedition gear, but none of them carried a pack.

Swain stepped forward. "Look who we have here," he said. "Our friends from the junior sabotage club. Looks like they made a wrong turn."

Frank looked around at the cliff behind him. There was no way to escape. "Listen," he said. "We need your help. My brother is missing."

"Really," Swain said, looking around suspiciously. "Why don't you tell him to come out from wherever he's hiding. I don't have time for any more games."

Frank was getting impatient. "Neither do we," he snapped back. "My brother fell into a crevasse hours ago. If we don't find him soon, it will be too late."

Hooper spoke up, apparently convinced by Frank's tone. "Don't you kids understand that these mountains are dangerous? We tried to tell you this was no place for beginners."

Frank felt his anger rising. "It wasn't my brother's fault," he shot back. "He fell into the crevasse when a rope ladder snapped underneath him. Somebody cut the ropes." He looked Swain squarely in the eye. "So don't talk to me about sabotage."

Swain seemed to be trying to decide whether to believe Frank's story. "Where and when did you lose your brother?" he asked finally.

Frank thought a moment. "More than five hours ago, to the north of here. If you're not going to help us find him, let us be on our way."

"If your brother really did fall into a crevasse," Swain answered, "I'm sorry to say his chances aren't good." He looked up at the dark sky. "I don't advise you to go out onto the glacier at night. If you do, there's a good chance that by morning your brother won't be the only one who winds up in a crevasse."

"If your brother's alive," the climber named Vadim said, "he should have dug himself a shelter in the snow by now and bedded down. That's the only way to survive a night in these mountains."

Frank refused to accept Swain's and Vadim's words. "I'm going after my brother, with or without your help," he said.

"Me, too," Mingma added.

Hooper clapped Swain on the shoulder. "Why don't Vadim and I go with them?" he suggested. "We'll watch them. There's a full moon rising. We'll head back to camp in a few hours."

Swain reluctantly agreed to Hooper's plan, and Frank and Mingma were relieved.

"Before we head out, we need to pick up our gear," Vadim told them. "We set up an advance camp not far from here."

They walked a short distance across the rocks and spotted the lights of the campsite, which was set up in a broad ravine below. As they approached the campsite, they could see several members of Swain's party confronting two Sherpas.

Mingma recognized them in the lamplight. "Uncle Pasang, Gyaltsen!" he exclaimed.

Swain's face turned to stone when he saw Pasang. "I knew you had to be around here somewhere," he said coldly. "As if you haven't already made enough trouble, you had to bring a bunch of teenagers into it. You ought to know better."

Pasang glared back at Swain. "We have done nothing to sabotage your expedition," he said evenly. "All we want to do is find the truth—before you bury it forever."

Swain bristled with anger. "You're the one who's trying to bury us!" he fumed. "Just like you did six years ago."

Frank was out of patience. Valuable time was being lost, and they weren't getting any closer to finding Joe. "Just hold it," he said, jumping between them. "Has it occurred to either of you that both of you may be missing the real culprit?"

For a moment they just stared at him. Then Swain broke the silence. "I suppose you're going to tell us who that is," he said sarcastically. "No, don't tell me, let me guess. I'll bet the yeti did it."

Joe's heart thumped from exertion. It was well after dark, and he was struggling to keep pace with the yeti as it made its way up the mountain. Despite the cold, Joe felt himself sweating. He was surprised at how far they'd gone and how fast they were moving.

The yeti seemed to be following a route it had used many times before. They had climbed up several steep pitches, in each case using fixed ropes and pitons already in place.

Joe guessed that they were moving along the northeast ridge they had seen that morning. The glacier where Joe had fallen into the crevasse was now behind and below them to the east.

Joe lost sight of the yeti. A large cornice

loomed ahead. This was a spot where wind had molded the snow and ice into an overhanging lip. Joe changed his course to steer clear of it, knowing that cornices could be unstable.

A minute later Joe spotted the figure of the yeti again, crouching above the cornice. He changed course to intercept it, holding his body low to the ground. But by the time he got to the cornice, there was no sign of the creature.

Expecting the yeti to jump him at any second, Joe crouched low and searched for possible hiding places. Then he crept to the edge of the cornice and took a look. He saw the glow of tents hundreds of feet below. Swain and his men must be camped there. He felt a tremendous wave of relief: he may have lost the yeti, but if he could make it down to the campsite, at least he could save himself.

But his mood took a hundred-and-eighty-degree turn seconds later when he spotted an object packed into the snow about ten feet from the edge of the cornice. He moved in for a closer look.

There was definitely some sort of package buried there. Three wires led from it to a timer, which had a digital display that blinked once per second. The timer was counting down from just over twenty-six minutes.

Joe's heart pounded with fear. He had a pretty good idea what he was looking at, but he still wanted to believe he was wrong. As he worked carefully to clear away the hard-packed snow with his axe, the object revealed itself to be a bundle of tubes neatly wrapped in canvas-type material.

When he saw the label—Danger/Explosives— it confirmed his worst suspicions.

Chapter

14

JOE KNEW HE HAD TO DO SOMETHING—and do it fast. There were at least fifteen sticks of dynamite in the package, and in less than half an hour, they were going to blow. When that happened, the cornice would break off, and hundreds of tons of snow and ice would go crashing down the mountain. The entire camp—and everyone in it—would be wiped out.

Joe struggled to remember everything he knew about defusing bombs. It wasn't too hard, because he didn't know much.

He bent over the bomb, examining it closely. He thought about cutting the wires, which might prevent the explosion—or set it off. If it blew, they would have to scrape him off the side of the mountain. Not that there would be anybody left to do the scraping, he thought grimly, thinking about the men camped below.

His brother and friends were somewhere out there in that frozen darkness, too. How big would the avalanche be, and would they be trapped in its path, too?

Joe racked his brains. Maybe if he shorted out the timer somehow, possibly by crossing one of the wires . . .

He was trying to decide whether crossing the wires was a good idea or a bad idea when something hit him hard from behind. He was knocked off balance and fell forward. Then he felt two powerful hairy arms encircling him.

He and the yeti landed together, sliding toward the edge of the cornice. Joe had the strange thought that the creature was fighting with human—rather than inhuman—strength. Still, the yeti was bigger and heavier, and Joe felt himself being overpowered.

Joe got one of his arms around his opponent and realized that the creature's hunched back was really a flap of loose fur that concealed a backpack. He also felt a long, hard object under the fur. It had to be that hunting rifle.

The yeti had him pinned now. In other circumstances, Joe might have been able to use his wrestling skills to break free, but the altitude and all the climbing had left him exhausted.

As they struggled close to the edge of the cornice, Joe saw an opportunity to free himself. "So, did both of your parents have this problem?" he asked. "Too bad your mother didn't take the time to shave more often. . . ."

In response, the creature gave Joe's neck a violent yank.

"I guess that means you speak English," Joe said to the phony yeti. "Why'd you decide to blow everybody up?" He was answered by another yank that left him gasping for air.

"I dare you to try that one more time," he panted, allowing his body to go almost limp. He winced as he felt the third sharp tug on his neck. The sudden pressure was followed by a brief release of force, and Joe chose that moment to spring. Tightening every muscle in his body, he thrust backward toward the edge of the cornice, throwing his attacker off balance. Locked together, they tumbled over the precipice.

Falling through the air, Joe had time to think that he'd done an awful lot of this sort of thing that day. Then they landed, rolling in the soft snow.

Joe struggled to his feet. He was momentarily free of his attacker. He looked back up to where the explosives were buried, but then the yeti rose to face him again. The clock was ticking, and Joe didn't have time to argue.

Ignoring his fur-clad assailant, Joe turned and

ran toward the camp below. The yeti followed, but Joe's agility kept him in the lead.

Not only was he racing the man in the yeti costume, but he was racing against the clock. By now he guessed there were no more than twenty minutes left.

Joe half ran, half fell down the side of the mountain, tumbling wildly over snowy terrain interspersed with rocks, expecting bullets to start landing around him at any moment. He wanted to look back but knew he didn't have a second to waste.

A bullet glanced off the rock beside him. He ducked and weaved as he scrambled on. Several more bullets followed. After one near miss, he hit the ground and began to slide.

The slide was unintentional at first, but then he remembered what Mingma had told him about the mountaineering technique of glissading, sliding down a slope in a seated or crouching position, using your ice ax as a rudder.

Joe tried it, and it worked. He made good progress, doing his best to zigzag to make himself harder to hit. He glissaded for several hundred feet to the end of the snow patch.

The rocks at the bottom offered good cover, but progress was a lot slower. Time was running out, and he still had at least half a mile to cover.

*   *   *

Meanwhile, at the campsite, Frank was facing down Roland Swain, Pasang, Gyaltsen, and all of Swain's men.

"You're too busy accusing each other to notice what's really going on," Frank said. "Were any of you up on the northeast ridge this afternoon?"

They all shook their heads. "Nobody should be up there," said Pasang.

"Well, somebody was," Frank said. "We saw him this afternoon." Mingma nodded agreement.

"Probably an animal," Thondup said.

"It wasn't an animal," Mingma answered. "He was walking erect. We saw him in the binoculars."

"All right," Swain cut in. "Maybe there was somebody on the ridge. That shouldn't come as much of a surprise. Every day I meet somebody else who's not supposed to be up here. It's becoming a regular tourist mecca."

Vadim spoke up. "Maybe it was your missing brother," he suggested to Frank.

Pasang looked around when he said this, noticing Joe's absence for the first time. "What happened to your brother?" he asked Frank.

"He fell into a crevasse," Frank said grimly. "Which is why we shouldn't be standing around here arguing. We should be out looking for him."

Pasang was distraught at this news. "This is my fault," he said. "I should never have allowed any of you to get involved in this."

Frank shook his head. "Joe came of his own

free will," he said. "But right now, the only thing that matters is that we all stop bickering and figure out what we can do to help Joe."

Pasang and Gyaltsen nodded in agreement. Several of Swain's men stepped forward. "We're willing to go out and have a look," one of them said.

"All right," Swain said. "But only volunteers in the search party."

Most of those present volunteered. Suddenly, the camp was a hive of activity as the volunteers readied their gear.

Within fifteen minutes the party was assembling in the center of the camp. Swain carefully outlined a rescue plan. Searchers would move in pairs for safety, combing the terrain in an organized fashion. All searchers would carry whistles and would reconvene every few hours to regroup, whether or not they had found anything.

"Remember that I'll be the one in charge of this search," Swain said. "Everyone follows my orders. And stay close. I'll still want some answers when we get back."

Standing next to Mingma, Frank pricked up his ears. "Did you hear that? It was a boom."

Mingma nodded. "Like thunder."

Frank was still listening. There was another sound now. Unlike thunder, this one didn't fade. It was coming from somewhere above them, and it kept on building.

Just then Joe Hardy burst into the campsite, looking like some kind of wild animal in the moonlight. Frank was horrified at his brother's condition. Joe's eyes were wild, his clothes torn, his face battered from exposure. He was moving his lips, too short of breath to speak.

Frank was even more horrified when Joe finally recovered enough to get a word out.

"Avalanche," Joe croaked.

No one but Frank heard him because by now the rumbling had grown to a loud roar. In less than a minute, hundreds of tons of ice and snow would come crashing down on them, and they would all suffocate under its weight.

Chapter

15

JOE MUSTERED HIS STRENGTH, took a deep breath, and let out a hoarse yell: "Avalanche!"

This time, everyone in the camp heard him, and they ran for their lives.

Frank and Joe scrambled toward the high rocks on the side of the ravine. They could feel the rumble of the avalanche in their chests.

Exhausted from his desperate race down the mountain, Joe couldn't keep up. Frank saw his brother lagging and went back to help him.

"Come on," Frank said, grabbing his brother's arm as a mass of falling snow came into view at the top of the ravine. A rock crashed by, narrowly missing them. Ahead of them, Mingma, Pasang, and Gyalt-sen reached the rocks and scrambled to safety.

Snow began to move under the Hardys' feet. They ran faster, struggling to reach higher ground before the full force of the avalanche hit the ravine.

Pasang and Gyaltsen reached out from the ledge above them, but the Hardys were too far away to grab hold, and they were swept into the torrent.

Still clutching Joe's arm, Frank saw a rocky outcrop below that they might be able to grab on to, if they could just keep from being dragged under before they reached it. He remembered reading that it was possible to survive an avalanche by "swimming" to stay on top. "Swim," he yelled to Joe, churning his arms and legs.

Out of the corner of his eye, he saw somebody running along the ledge above them. Then a rope flew over his head and landed between them. Both of them grabbed the rope and held on for dear life.

They saw Mingma straining on the end of the rope and Swain leaping to join him. Together, they hauled the Hardys through the current to safety.

"Thanks for the lift," Frank gasped once they stood on the rocks. "I thought we were dead."

They quickly scrambled to the highest point on the ledge, where all the survivors had assembled. They were standing on an island of rock as thousands of tons of snow, ice, and rock tumbled down on either side of them.

Gradually, the roar subsided. The mountain was finally still again, but nobody said anything for several moments. The raw power of the avalanche had stunned them into silence.

Joe's mind was still racing to make sense of it all. He heard Frank ask if everyone was okay. A quick head count revealed that everyone had made it to safety—thanks to Joe's warning.

Gradually, Joe felt all eyes settling on him. "Explosives" was all he could say at first. He pointed back up the mountain. "Somebody wired a cornice to blow, right above camp."

Pasang stared at Joe. "Somebody caused this avalanche?" he said.

Joe nodded. "The yeti did it . . . I mean, somebody dressed as a yeti. But I don't know who."

"How did you find out?" Swain asked. "You were supposed to be trapped in a crevasse."

Joe recounted his escape from the crevasse, how he discovered the hidden campsite, followed the "yeti," and uncovered the explosives.

"Whoever it is, this guy is armed and dangerous," Joe said.

"Frankly, your story sounds crazy," Swain said. "But your warning did save us. At this point, I guess I'm ready to believe just about anything."

Swain offered his hand to Pasang. "I guess this could mean I've been wrong about you, too," he said. "I'm sorry."

Pasang accepted Swain's hand.

"Now that we're all on the same side," Frank said, "maybe we can finally solve this mystery."

Swain barked out more orders, and the group mobilized. Since they had been about to set out on a rescue mission when the avalanche hit, most of the men were carrying backpacks with bivouac sacks, cold-weather gear, and other emergency equipment. But the tents and most of the long-term supplies were completely buried.

"We'll bivouac here for the night," Swain said. "In the morning, we'll head out in two groups. Hooper, Vadim, and I will go after our friend in the yeti costume. Everyone else will return to the main base camp to pick up supplies."

Pasang and Gyaltsen stepped forward. "We're going with you," Pasang said firmly. "We have just as much at stake in this as you do."

"Fair enough," Swain said. "You've earned it."

"You'll never find the hidden campsite without me," Joe said.

"Where Joe goes, I go," Frank said.

"Count me in, too," Mingma added.

Swain rolled his eyes. "This is starting to sound more like a picnic in the Alps. Why don't we just send out an invitation to the yeti? Then he can come on in and join us, and we won't have to go looking for him."

The next morning they broke camp at first light. One group set out for base camp as planned. The Hardys and their friends went with the other group, following Joe back to the yeti's campsite.

"Let's backtrack the way I came last night," Joe said. "We can climb back up to the northeast ridge, then work our way across and down."

The day was bright and clear, and they made good progress along the ridge. Around mid-morning, they reached the spot where Joe had first come upon the yeti's footprints. Soon the campsite came into view as expected. It looked deserted.

They had nearly reached the tent when Joe spotted someone stealing away. "He's getting away," he said, and shot off in pursuit, followed by Frank and the others. After a thirty-yard sprint, Joe easily brought the man down with a flying tackle. He knew right away that this wasn't the man in the yeti outfit.

Joe pulled the man to his feet, and Frank yanked off his hood to reveal a pointy-nosed man with eyes that darted nervously as he squirmed around.

Joe recognized him immediately. "It's Jumpy from the teahouse," he said.

"You know this man?" Swain asked.

"We met him once," Frank said. "He was snooping outside Pasang's house back in Patan."

"You must be mistaken," Jumpy snarled. "I

haven't been near Patan or Kathmandu for months."

"Make sure he's not armed," Joe suggested.

Frank frisked him quickly. He felt something hard under the man's jacket. As he yanked open the zipper, his eye caught the glimmer of metal.

"You haven't been in Kathmandu lately, huh?" Frank asked. "Then where did you get this?" He grabbed the object and held it up triumphantly. Mingma's and Pasang's eyes widened when they saw that the gold object in Frank's hand was Pasang's watch.

"You stole this watch from my bedroom and pushed my father down the stairs," Mingma said.

The man was still defiant. "I don't know what you're talking about," he insisted.

Swain stepped forward, a controlled rage burning in his eyes. With one arm, he lifted Jumpy up by the neck. "Last night someone set off an avalanche that buried our camp and almost killed us. I'm going to give you five seconds to start talking before I snap your neck like a twig."

Jumpy squirmed in Swain's grip, fear in his eyes. Even the Hardys couldn't tell whether or not Swain was bluffing.

"I admit I stole the watch," Jumpy said. "I also pushed his father down the stairs, but that was an accident."

Mingma's eyes flared, but he said nothing as Swain finally lowered the man to the ground.

Jumpy quickly backed away from Swain, massaging his neck, and then turned to Mingma.

"I broke into your room hoping to find something that would lead me to your uncle," he explained. "I had seen him give you the watch the night of the lecture, outside the Annapurna Hotel, so when I found the watch pieces and the note in your drawer, I knew that it was an important clue."

Pasang interrupted. "Why were you looking for me? I don't know you."

The man hesitated. "I wanted to keep you from coming anywhere near this mountain," he confessed. "I wanted to keep all of you away from this mountain," he said to the group.

"Wait a minute," Swain said. "You said you were at the Annapurna Hotel the night of my lecture. So you're the one who tried to kill me in my room that night." The big mountaineer stepped forward menacingly.

Jumpy's eyes twitched with fear. "I never meant to kill you. Just to scare you off."

"And the avalanche?" Gyaltsen asked. "That was just to scare us, too?"

"That was not me. I swear it. I was being paid to scare you off, but that was all. I never thought things would go this far."

"He's telling the truth about not being the one who set the explosives last night," Joe said. "I'm sure of it."

Frank folded his arms. "Start from the beginning. Who are you, and who are you working for?"

"My name is Jang Bu," the man began.

"You're the one Bimbahadur talked about," Gyaltsen said. His eyes narrowed. "You threatened him and then burned down his home."

"Bimbahadur was supposed to keep his mouth shut," Jang Bu said.

"You still haven't told us who hired you," Swain said.

Jang Bu shifted nervously. "Six years ago, while many of you were busy trying to climb Yeti's Tower, we were also here, but not to climb the mountain. My employer wanted—"

He never finished. A shot rang out, glancing off a rock behind them. Everyone dove for cover. Everyone except Jang Bu, who tried to run in the opposite direction. He made it only a few steps before another shot rang out, and he crumpled to the ground in a heap.

Chapter

16

THE HARDYS AND THEIR PARTY crouched behind the rocks as the shots came at regular intervals. They seemed to be coming from somewhere back up the trail. They could see Jang Bu lying where he had fallen. He hadn't moved.

Finally, the shooting stopped. Frank waited several minutes, then held up his backpack as a decoy. Nothing happened. He looked at Joe.

Joe shrugged and said, "I guess we can't sit here all day."

Cautiously, the Hardys emerged from the rocks and made their way to where Jang Bu lay in the snow, blood oozing from a wound in his head.

Joe knelt beside the fallen man and put a hand on his neck. "No pulse," he said. "He's dead."

139

He had a hollow feeling in his chest. Jang Bu had attacked them several times, but that didn't mean he wanted him shot down in cold blood.

Frank stared at the corpse in the snow, then back up to where the shots came from. "Whoever did this is going to pay," he said grimly.

"He can't have gone far," Joe said. "We can pick up the trail if we hurry."

"We?" Swain repeated. "Not we. I'm going after him, alone." The others started to object, but he held up his hand. "Hold it," he said. "There's a madman up there doing his best to kill us. I've seen too many people die already. This is my fight. My stepbrothers were the only family I had left."

"Gyaltsen and I are going with you," Pasang said. "We also have a stake in this. We also watched our friends die six years ago."

All the while, Frank was scanning the slope above them. "Look," he said suddenly, raising his binoculars. Following his gaze, the others could make out a figure moving rapidly on the ridge above. Almost as soon as they looked, it disappeared out of sight.

"Let's get him," Joe said, starting off for the ridge. Frank, Mingma, and the others followed.

There was no one in sight by the time they reached the spot where they had seen the figure. But there were plenty of footprints.

"These are our tracks from this morning," Joe

said. "No way to tell whether our yeti friend's tracks are mixed in with them."

"I can guess where he's headed," Mingma said.

"The Chomolungma face," Frank said.

Swain turned to the Hardys and Mingma. "At the risk of repeating myself," he said, "you three ought to head back down to base camp. Chomolungma is way beyond your skill level."

"Nothing doing," Joe answered. "We can handle it. We've learned a lot in the last few days."

"Down here, it's just the foothills," Pasang told him. "Up there, the altitude alone can kill you. You need time to acclimatize."

"We won't go all the way to the top," Frank said. "But we're going as far as Chomolungma. And that's final."

They set out without further discussion. By early afternoon they had made their way back up the northeast ridge to where the cornice was blown up the night before. They continued along the ridge approaching the top of the horn. This was the "false summit" Joe had spotted the day before.

Frank, Joe, and Mingma were near exhaustion. They were above twenty thousand feet now. Sweat dripped from their brows, and they were short of breath all the time. They kept moving on pure determination.

From the top of the horn, Frank and Joe got a good look at the true summit of Yeti's Tower for the first time. Across a narrow valley, a sheer wall of rock and snow rose up to blot out the horizon. They had to crane their necks skyward to see where the pinnacle culminated in a glistening white point.

The wall of rock in front of them was almost a thousand feet high.

"That's it—the Chomolungma face," Mingma said.

Joe had butterflies in his stomach as he surveyed the face. Large sections were covered with ice. There were a few ledges and cracks, but in most places he couldn't see any handholds.

"How do you climb something that smooth?" he asked.

"It's not completely smooth," Pasang replied. "There are cracks."

"The central crack offers the best route," Gyaltsen explained, pointing to it. "But it doesn't reach all the way to the top. You must do a pendulum swing on the rope to the next crack for the final pitch."

That night, they camped in the valley at the base of Chomolungma. It was still dark when they woke the next morning, but preparations were already underway.

The plan was to divide the face into a series of separate pitches. Swain and Vadim would lead up the first pitch, fixing ropes as they went. Hooper and Mingma would follow, then Frank and Joe. Pasang and Gyaltsen would bring up the rear.

Climbing up, Frank found that in some places the crack was wide enough for him to fit half of his body into if he turned sideways. In other spots, he had to use a lieback position, pulling against the crack with one or both hands while pressing with his feet to produce counterforce.

It was exhausting work. Between pitches, Frank had time to wonder where the yeti was. He hated to think what would happen if somebody started shooting at them now.

By late morning they had climbed the central crack as high as possible. Swain and Vadim had already made the pendulum swing over to the next crack and were continuing upward.

Luckily, the central crack branched off at the top in the direction they needed to swing. This allowed them to fix the rope out on this branch and then climb back down to give themselves some length of rope to swing.

Joe went first. The rope supported him as he sidestepped in a broad arc across the vertical rock, an eight-hundred-fifty-foot drop below his feet. He didn't make it far enough on the first swing, so he ran back as far as he could in the other direction to give himself momentum. On the second swing, he made it.

Now it was Frank's turn. He gave himself more

rope than Joe had taken, hoping to swing in a wider arc and make it across on the first attempt.

All the same, he missed on his first try. Like Joe, he sidestepped as far as he could on the backswing, but because of the extra rope, he swung in a lower, broader arc.

At the height of his backswing, his eyes locked on a horrendous sight.

He had only seen it for a moment, but there was no mistaking what it was.

Hanging from a belay rope attached to the cliff, half frozen into the surrounding ice, was a human corpse.

Chapter

17

FRANK HAD ONLY CAUGHT A GLIMPSE for a fraction of a second, but the dead man's features would be forever etched in his memory. The elements had taken their toll. The eyes had been reduced to sunken pits, the skin was like blackened leather, and the teeth were exposed in an eternal grimace.

Somehow, Frank managed to complete his swing back across the face and find a hold. Above him, his brother had wedged his arm into the crack to hold himself in place.

"You look like you just saw a ghost," Joe said. "Hang in there. We're almost at the top."

"Joe, I think I just found one of the Waldmann twins," Frank answered, his voice numb, his face pale. "Frozen into the side of the mountain."

Joe looked at him, not sure what to say.

"I just want to get to the top," Frank said. "Then we can talk about it."

Within fifteen minutes they had reached the top of the face. There they rested on a gentle, snow-covered incline, dotted with boulders. Like a frozen wave, a massive cornice of snow hung above them.

The Hardys knew that this gentle slope offered only an illusion of safety. This was the spot where the avalanche had started six years ago, sweeping nine unlucky members of the Waldmann expedition nearly a thousand feet to their deaths.

Frank could barely remember the last part of the climb. He tried to focus on the fact that they were thousands of feet up on one of the highest mountains in the world and that there was a madman with a rifle out there somewhere. But all he could think about was the dead man's face. He told Swain and the others what he had seen.

Swain lowered himself down on a rope to see for himself. He reappeared over the edge a few minutes later. "It's Luther," he said in a blank voice. "He's been frozen there for six years." He stared at the ground. "I'll have to go back down and cut him out of the ice."

Hooper volunteered to help him. Swain took another rope and secured it to a nearby boulder. "The rest of you, be ready to haul up on this rope," he said. "We'll give you three quick tugs when we're ready."

Swain and Hooper disappeared over the edge. It took them more than an hour to complete their gruesome task, but finally the signal came. Joe took his turn at the front of the rope, pulling hand over hand, a few inches at a time.

Finally, the frozen remains of Luther Waldmann came over the top. Joe took one look and turned away. He had seen enough.

As Vadim was wrapping the body in a poncho, a shot rang out. They all threw themselves down behind the rocks. Joe saw Vadim clutching his arm, blood on his fingers. He had been hit. Swain and Hooper still hadn't made it back up off the cliff.

Joe peered up between the rocks and stiffened when he saw the barrel of a gun just a short distance away. It was pointed right at them. He ducked as another bullet flew past.

Frank was crouched at Joe's right. The sound of the rifle shots snapped him out of his daze. Suddenly, he was full of deadly purpose.

"Cover me," he told Joe and Mingma, without offering any suggestions about how. Then he was gone, crouched down, running between the rocks.

Joe and Mingma began hurling rocks and insults, doing anything they could to draw their attacker's attention away from Frank, who was darting among the rocks on their right.

Frank kept moving until he had worked his way behind the gunman, then he stopped. There was about twenty feet of open ground between Frank and the shooter. Chances were that the man would hear Frank coming and have time to turn and fire.

From where they were sitting, Joe and Mingma recognized Frank's predicament. "Maybe I can get to him from the other direction," Mingma whispered.

"There's no cover over there," Joe said, but Mingma was already running.

Frank saw Mingma run out into the open and watched in horror as the gunman carefully took aim at his friend. Frank had no choice. He ran full speed toward the gunman, who wheeled at the last instant. Frank sprang like a tiger, knocking the gun away with a sweep of his left hand and chopping the man down with a swift blow to the neck from his right.

Gasping for breath, Frank grabbed the yeti mask and pulled it off, revealing a square-jawed man with blond hair. The others crowded around. Swain and Hooper were the last to arrive, having just reached the top of the cliff.

"Luther didn't die in any accident," Swain said grimly. "He was murdered. There's a bullet hole in his skull." Without another word, Swain picked the rifle up from where it lay on the ground and put it against the captured man's forehead. He was ready to pull the trigger, but Pasang stepped forward and snatched the gun out of his hand.

"Wait," Pasang said. "We don't even know who he is."

"I think I do," Frank said. "I've seen pictures of him. It's Richard Skelton, owner of the Yeti Adventure Travel Company, where Jang Bu worked."

The man looked at Frank in surprise as Swain advanced on him again and said, "Whatever your name is, you'd better explain yourself—and fast." Swain grabbed him and started dragging him toward the precipice.

"All right, enough," the man said. "I am Richard Skelton. But I never murdered your stepbrother. It was an accident. I'm a big-game hunter, and I've spent years in this country, trying to bag the ultimate trophy—the yeti."

Joe couldn't believe his ears. "You're trying to shoot a creature that doesn't even exist?"

"The yeti does exist," Skelton insisted. "Six years ago, I stalked one right to this spot. I had him in my sights."

"Only it was Luther Waldmann," Frank said. "You shot him by mistake."

Skelton nodded and continued, "I don't know how it happened. The visibility was poor, he was covered with snow. There *was* a yeti. It was just bad luck that Luther showed up when he did."

Joe stared at Skelton in disbelief, trying to decide whether the man should be arrested, committed, or just pushed off the cliff.

"As soon as it happened, Luther's brother came at me. I dodged, and he went over the cliff. They were still roped together, and he dragged his brother's body with him."

"So that's how Luther ended up hanging there," Frank said. "The rope must have snagged on something. The bodies were out of reach but not out of sight."

Skelton nodded. "The rest of their party was on their way down. I could hear them coming."

"So you caused the avalanche, to bury the evidence," Joe guessed.

"All I did was move the belay rope the Waldmanns set for the rest of the party. That way, the rest of them wouldn't see the bodies. I guess I moved it too close to the cornice. One of the climbers slipped, and the whole thing gave way. There was nothing I could do to stop the avalanche."

"You were the one who was evacuated by helicopter!" Joe exclaimed, remembering the Ministry of Tourism records that Mingma's friend Pertemba had shown them. "You knew the bodies were still up there. If anybody ever found them, it might point to you. Then Pasang showed up at Swain's lecture and made his accusations."

Skelton nodded. "It was too close to home,"

he said. "Jang Bu was just supposed to throw you off the trail, but he bungled it."

"So you came after us in your yeti getup with your elephant gun," Swain said. "Nice try. Tie him up," he barked. Then he turned to Hooper and said, "Let's go back to find Ernst."

The two mountaineers checked their ropes, then dropped down over the edge to search for the body of the second Waldmann twin. They found it wedged into a crack one hundred feet below where Frank had found Luther, and they carefully hauled it back up. A few of the men turned away while the others watched in silence as they laid the bodies of the twins side by side and covered them with a two-man tent.

"Gentlemen," Swain said, turning to Frank, Joe, and Mingma after a brief pause. "We've still got a mountain to climb."

"We'll escort the corpses and the prisoner back to Jumla," Mingma said. "That way your team can complete its assault on the summit."

"No way," Swain said. "You three have earned the right to join us at the top, and I'm not going to let you squirm out of it." He nodded toward the two covered bodies. "You'd be dishonoring the memory of two great mountain climbers."

Frank glanced up at the summit. "He's right, Mingma. We bagged our yeti—now let's go conquer his mountain."

Frank and Joe's next case:

Chet has won a ticket to ride from the International Ballooning Club, and the Hardys have learned that it could also be a ticket to disaster. A series of suspicious accidents have plagued the show, and with the upcoming Lift Challenge offering a $100,000 prize, the organizers of the event have received an anonymous threat: "Pay up or die!" Frank and Joe recognize the gravity of the situation: What goes up must come down. But will anyone get hurt when the fall comes? The boys launch a high-stakes, high-risk investigation in search of the extortionist, knowing that the warning is more than hot air. At these heights, a tiny flame could turn one of the balloons into a ball of fire . . . in *Sky High*, Case #113 in The Hardy Boys Casefiles™.